MW01127889

GODFATHER OF ATLANTA 2

COLE HART

Cole Hart
SIGNATURE NOVELS

UF
Hart

Godfather Of Atlanta 2

Copyright © 2020 by Cole Hart

All rights reserved.

Published in the United States of America.

All rights reserved. No part of this publication may be reproduced, distributed, or transmitted in any form or by any means, including photocopying, recording, or other electronic or mechanical methods, without the prior written permission of the publisher, except in the case of brief quotations embodied in critical reviews and certain other noncommercial uses permitted by copyright law. For permission requests, please contact: www.colehartsignature.com

This is a work of fiction. Names, characters, places, and incidents either are the products of the author's imagination or are used fictitiously. Any resemblance of actual persons, living or dead, businesses, companies, events, or locales is entirely coincidental. The publisher does not have any control and does not assume any responsibility for author or third-party websites or their content.

The unauthorized reproduction or distribution of this copyrighted work is a crime punishable by law. No part of the book may be scanned, uploaded to or downloaded from file sharing sites, or distributed in any other way via the Internet or any other means, electronic, or print, without the publisher's permission. Criminal copyright infringement, including infringement without monetary gain, is investigated by the FBI and is punishable by up to five years in federal prison and a fine of $250,000 (www.fbi.gov/ipr/).

This book is licensed for your personal enjoyment only. Thank you for respecting the author's work.

Published by Cole Hart Signature, LLC.

Mailing List

To stay up to date on new releases, plus get information on contests, sneak peeks, and more,

Go To The Website Below...

www.colehartsignature.com

1

W ho cares if Hammer was rumored to have once held the title of 'Killa' or whatever? Cats from all walks of life carried that same title on their head, and they lurked all around the city of Atlanta. Different features, countries and nationalities. Everybody knew he was a multi-millionaire, and to a few, the response was, 'who cares?' That was the attitude of other multi-millionaires who flooded the streets, and Six-Nine was at the top of the list of those who didn't care.

Hammer didn't seem angered at all by the disturbing phone call that he'd received only minutes go. He sat casually behind his mahogany desk as if he was the President of the United States. Thick burnt orange carpet was underneath his feet, stretching from wall-to-wall. His eyes swept his office and paused at a four-foot glass statue of a naked woman pressed against a naked man. Then his eyes shifted to the floor-to-ceiling windows that gave the entire eastside of his office an overwhelming view of the city. He came out of his thoughts and reached for his office phone, gripped it, and realized that his heart rate had sped up. This was something that didn't happen

too often. Maybe the phone call *did* rock him. Disturbed him a
little.

Hammer stared at the phone and grinded his back teeth.
Six-Nine flashed before him in a fine tuned vision. His words
cut him like a Gillette Mach 3 razor. "A fuck nigga." he whispered into the air. "He called me a fuck nigga."

He stood so quickly, the chair nearly flipped over backwards. The cordless phone still gripped in his hand. He was
dressed in a two-piece chocolate linen suit, matching gators,
with rose gold buckles and cuff links. His hard fiery eyes darted
around the office. A deep breath here, another one there, as he
moved toward the window and noticed that the city was
growing right before his eyes. Skyscrapers were getting taller,
and more steel frames were popping up everywhere. He looked
up to the clear blue skies and thought about how beautiful life
had become from his position at the top of his game, and surely
how it will be for years to come.

In his rise to power over the last few years, he'd heard about
the Mexican cartels and the Black Mafia Family who did the
majority of the street construction work around the city. He was
familiar with that; it was one of the reasons he kept his ear to
the street. But why in the hell hadn't he ever heard about the
Black Cartel? He would definitely tumble that around in his
head until he found out.

Hammer didn't take anything too lightly. Not even the
peons. He felt like he'd slipped up somewhere. That angered
him too. He quickly punched a number on his phone.

Vincent answered on the second ring. "How may I help
you?"

"You ain't got shit betta to do besides sit around da' house
and screen ya' calla ID every time da' phone rang?"

"Actually, I got two bad young bitches over here poppin'
pills and givin' me head until further notice." He took a deep
breath. "Pimps up."

Hammer had to laugh at that one, and then the fun was over. He asked Vincent, "Whatcha' know about the Black Cartel records?"

"New crew of young cats runnin' round da city." Vincent spoke into the phone. Then he said, "Anything I need ta' check into?"

"Yeah, I believe you do, gangsta'." Hammer shot back. "Mainly, I want you ta' get da' status on dat dude, Six-Nine."

"Six-Nine?" Vincent asked in a questioning tone, as if he was asking himself. "I remember that name. Da tall young nigga from da' partment. Yeah...Yeah." Vincent's voice rose. "Yeah, he on Rice street fa' bout five ah six bodies or somethin' like dat. Shawdy fucked up."

Hammer nodded, still standing before the window. He saw a white news helicopter zip by before he spoke into the phone. "Well, I jus' got a call from dude, and I'm gonna assume he's surfaced again. And da' motha'fucka' don dropped his nuts again." He nearly shouted as he moved away from the window and snatched two sheets of Kleenex from a box that sat upon a mantelpiece.

"He ain't nothin' but a peon to us, gangsta."

Hammer heard every word that Vincent was saying to him. He moved back around the desk and sat down in his leather swivel. He wiped his sweaty palms with the Kleenex and tossed them in the trash.

"Check into it fa' me anyway. Sissy ass nigga startin' to get under my skin." Hammer growled in a low tone.

"Gangsta, don't blow yo' cool fuckin wit' no lame." Vincent said, then added, "You doin' too goddamn good out here, you bout ta' get married. Ya' bad ass son 'bout ta' come home. You gotcha weight up. From here to heaven, gangsta. These niggas don't wanna see us."

The words flowed from Vincent's mouth as if they had been rehearsed for a scene in a Spike Lee film.

Hammer shrugged a little. "I'm glad you know how to make it sound good."

He took another deep breath and his palms began to sweat again. A knock at the office door caught his attention. Two quick taps. Just as his eyes cut up toward the door, it came open. A young looking female poked her head inside. Her hair was in tiny neat dreads, and she wore just enough makeup to enhance her seductive eyes and beautiful face.

She gave Hammer a smile and motioned her small hand like a mouth opening and closing. She moved her lips. "I need to talk to you."

Hammer held up a finger to her, and then he spoke back into the phone in a calmer tone. "Get a location on dis' lame for me. And dats at all cost, then I'll send Kangoma to you."

"So he back from Africa?" Vincent asked from the other end.

"Yeah, he home. Well, his new home." There was a short pause between them. "Talk to you later." He hung up and waved the girl in.

She sat down in one of the two chairs in front of his desk. The girl was a young intern who was hired to help with whatever needed to be done around the studio. Clean, pick up food, order food, and a few other things here and there. Her main thing was also to scout the streets for new talent.

"Wuss'up, Bird?" Hammer said in a powerful, but even tone of voice.

He leaned back in his chair and locked eyes with her. Total silence fell over the office, then the sound of the water gulping from the pure water machine in the corner filled the room.

Bird's facial features casually turned; she looked more serious than he'd ever seen her. She spat her problem at him like she was throwing up from too much Patron. "I need to borrow five bands, man. It's an emergency, and I ain't gon' tell you no lie."

"Okay." Hammer said sharply. He leaned forward and placed his elbows on his desk. "What's the emergency?"

Bird leaned in and cleared her throat. "Alright," she began. "My auntie, Ms. Mary. Everybody call her Ms. Mary. You know her, dontcha'? Da' same Ms. Mary dat' use ta' sell candy apples on da' Westside. Anyway, her house is condemned, and I don't want her living like dat. I'm jus' tryna help her move."

Hammer was listening hard, and the story was interesting. He continued to stare at Bird. He didn't think she was lying, then again, he couldn't be sure. He finally said, "So five grand is gonna handle everything?"

"Yeah, basically. I got fo' grand myself that I'm gonna use to help her out."

"What else do Ms. Mary do?"

"Like what?" she asked. Her facial muscles tightened up a little.

"Dope! She use or sell?"

Bird frowned and shook her head. "Nah... She drank a lil bit though."

He opened both hands as if to say that he didn't have a problem with that. Then he nodded in agreement. "First thing in the mornin'."

A bright smile spread across her face. She stood in a professional manner and extended her manicured hand. "Thank you," she said.

Hammer stood with her, still holding her hand. A quick thought ran across his mind. He released her hand and casually walked around to the front of his desk. "Let me ask you a question..."

Bird paused briefly, her shoulders back and her head slightly tilted backwards, staring up into his eyes. "I'm listenin'," she said.

"Have you ever heard of a crew that call themselves the Black Cartel?"

Bird's eyebrows bunched together as her mind tumbled in thought. She knew she'd heard the name before from somewhere, then out of the blue, she said, "Lil Willie, from da' South. I think that supposed to be his crew." She put a hand on her hip.

Hammer shook his head. "I neva heard of him." He leaned to the left, allowing his body to relax from his right side. "Grab a seat." He said, and motioned towards one of the leather stuffed sofas. "You got a minute?"

She nodded quickly and gave him a 'why wouldn't I?' look. She moved to her seat, and for the next twenty minutes, she explained everything to Hammer that she knew about Lil Willie. Not one time did she mention Six-Nine's name. Then again, she didn't have to. Hammer's mind was made up.

2

Vincent lived in a private gated community on the upper end of Cascade road, only five minutes away from the 285 intersection. The community was equipped with single, two, and three story estates with price tags starting at a half million dollars. His estate was a two story gray brick with large windows and a three-car garage. The driveway was asphalt and the home sat on four acres of land.

In the driveway, there were two cars. One was a glossy black Lexus 430 Sports Coupe with hard top convertible. The other one was an old model Bentley that was midnight blue in color. Everything factory original.

Inside the house, Vincent and his son, Vincent Jr., sat in the kitchen at a marble top table across from each. The older Vincent was wrapped in a blue terry cloth Polo robe. His eyes squinted against the streaming cigarette smoke. Vincent Jr. was fully dressed in Red Monkey jeans and a matching shirt with Red Monkey splashed across his chest. His lady friend in Vegas had sent it to him a few weeks back.

Vincent Jr. downed half a glass of orange juice and snacked

on salted almonds, while watching his old man smoke uncontrollably on his Newport. He looked him in his eyes and asked, "What Hamma talkin' bout?"

Vincent drained the remainder of the orange juice from his glass. The melting ice cubes rattled as they hit the bottom. He belched and took another long pull from his cigarette. Smoke streamed from his nose and mouth. Finally, he mashed the cigarette out in the ashtray and stared at his son. "Hamma wanna kill dat boy," he said, then added, "I was under da impression dat he was still on Rice Street."

Vincent Jr. shook his head. "Nah. Pimp out. Word on da street is dem niggas built a team on Rice Street and they got homes out."

Vincent nodded, then asked, "So what, you fuck wit dude and them?"

"To a certain extent. You know a lot of 'em be in Summer Hill, and they got da Box on lock wit da work." He shrugged. "Yeah, Six Nine on da loose. He on some otha shit too."

"Well, you need to get at dude. See what da business is." Vincent said.

"I'm assuming he feeling some type of way. But somthin' got to be arranged."

"Arranged, like what?"

"I don't know. Something thorough." Vincent Jr. leaned back, reached in his waistline, came out with a black Desert Eagle, and set it on the table between them.

"If dat's what it take to get da matter resolved," Vincent said as he cut his eyes down at the weapon.

He looked back at his son again, lost in his own thoughts for a minute. The thought of his son stepping up to the plate and showing his hands of loyalty filled him with pride. He was looking in his eyes now, nearly boring into his soul. *It's running through his veins.* Vincent said to himself. He knew he was getting up in age, and at fifty something, surely the retirement stage was near. He wasn't able to run the streets like he'd once done twenty and thirty years ago. "On yo word, you sho you can handle dis?"

Vincent Jr. cocked his head to the side and bunched his eyebrows together as if he couldn't believe that his old man had questioned his ability. "You got my word."

Vincent cracked a smile and slowly nodded. His eyes never left his son's stare. "Seven days?"

"Dats reasonable."

It took Vincent Jr. more than a week to run Six-Nine down, and it definitely wasn't an easy task. He'd made calls, majority of them to some certified elite major street millionaires and gangsters that knew Six-Nine personally. He'd made calls back to his father, then their calls were relayed to Hammer. Then the calls were relayed to the Governor, who also had to put his word on it.

Other organizations across Atlanta reached out for the cause. "My word is all I got." "That's on everything I love." "Our lil sisters went to school together." "My mother cooked at your Grandmother's funeral."

Those were just some of the so-called loyalty statements that were passed around the city so that Six-Nine and Hammer could have a sit down. Hammer had made a promise to himself that if he'd ever so much as had a dream about him, he would murder him. Now the situation had changed slightly, not enough though. Nobody really knew what Hammer had crawling up his sleeves. One of his own famous quotes was, *you got to cut the grass to see the snakes. Then chop the snake's head.*

Three more days passed, and the meeting day arrive. It had been arranged at an exclusive restaurant called Bones. Everyone pulled into the parking lot in expensive vehicles. Hammer, Kangoma, Vincent and Vincent Jr., rode together in a stretch limousine, all casually dressed for the event. Kangoma eased the limousine up to the curb of the five-star restaurant in Buckhead. He got out, wearing a triple black tuxedo underneath his jacket. He moved around the limo where one of two valets were standing. He shook hands with a six-foot two Jamaican with dreads and hazel eyes.

"How you doin?" Kangoma asked him.

The dread nodded with a confident smile. Without a word, Kangoma handed him a set of keys. They pretended to shake hands again. Kangoma clapped the dread on his back and whispered in his ear. "Everybody in place?"

The dread nodded. "Fifteen in da restaurant. Five out here in da parking lot."

Without another word, Kangoma opened the rear door of the limo. Hammer stepped out in linen pants, charcoal colored shirt, and matching Louis Vuitton shoes. He scanned the parking lot with an intense stare. When he spotted the dread, he instantly knew that he was a head soldier of his crew. Their eyes briefly met then he stepped to the side and waited for Vincent to exit the limousine.

Vincent stepped out, casually dressed as well, and then came Vincent Jr. in an expensive tailored suit. Everyone shook Kangoma's hand, and then they were escorted inside.

The aroma of the exotic dishes filled the air. Hammer's name and face was very familiar as he, Vincent and Vincent Jr. were escorted to a private room in the restaurant. There was a huge round table made of white marble, which was big enough to seat sixteen people. Floor-to-ceiling ivory drapes hung open, and beautiful chandeliers illuminated the room. They were all seated next to one another, and five minutes later, an attractive female entered in hip clinging slacks, low heels, and long confident strides. She wore dreads and a light touch of makeup.

Hammer stood as she got close to the table. He extended his hand and she gripped it firmly, giving him steady eye contact. No smile, straight business. "The Governor has arrived," she said calmly.

3

Back in the parking lot, the Governor arrived in a new model steel-colored Rolls Royce Phantom Drophead Coupe with suicide doors. A black Hummer in front and another one behind accompanied him. Each one of them had dark tinted windows that made it hard to see inside.

From the first Hummer, three guys emerged, appearing to be young goons, all of them dressed in urban gear. They posted near the front of the Rolls Royce. Three more goons exited the second Hummer; they looked more cautious and anxious, and moved swiftly. One of them opened the rear door of the Rolls Royce.

The Governor swung his legs out first, then the bottom of a cane hit the paved parking lot, and finally, he stepped out. His eyes slowly searched the parking lot. He was very cautious, dressed in a dark colored two-piece suit and crocodile skin shoes. After a few handshakes, he was also escorted inside the restaurant.

When the Governor reached the private room where Hammer and the Vincents waited, Hammer stood and embraced him. "J.W." Hammer said. "Wuss with the cane? Them bad ass feet bothering you again?"

The Governor smirked slightly and Hammer and shook his head.

Vincent stood and hugged the table along with the six goons that the Governor had brought with him. Everybody shook hands and exchanged casual nods. No more than two minutes later, two more guys appeared. They were both casually dressed and stood well over six feet tall. Huge diamonds hung from their earlobes. They were cousins, and both of them were millionaires from east Atlanta. Hammer knew of the cousins, but he had never met them in person. They were much younger than he was, maybe in the age range of Young Hollywood.

Hammer greeted them both with a firm handshake and a brief nod. They sat as well. Three more minutes went by, and five young gentlemen entered the private room along with two beefy looking women who could've passed for power forwards in the WNBA. They all walked and acted the same way. They represented another notorious clique that called themselves The Trained 2 Go Clique. The private room was beginning to fill up.

Hammer leaned in closer to the Governor and whispered in his ear. "I don't think he's gonna show up."

The Governor looked at Hammer. "You don't think he's already dead, do you?"

Hammer grinned a little. "Damn sho would be nice, and it'll save me a lot of work."

The Governor scanned the menu and then told Hammer, "Sauteed wild salmon with the braised white bean soup. No Bacon."

"Mothafucka', do I look like a waiter?"

A convoy of SUVs followed one behind another on Piedmont Rd, carrying at least forty members of the Black Cartel. Six-Nine rode in a black Excursion, sipping on syrup and a thirteen hundred dollar bottle of Chateau-Paulet Cognac. He was on his phone trying to locate his right hand man, LC. Now LC was known to disappear with females and get lost for a couple of days. Six-Nine knew this, but he wasn't angry because he'd only had half of his crew with him. He fired up a Newport and dialed LC's number again, just as they were turning into the parking lot of Bones. This time, the call went straight to voicemail.

"How many times I got to tell dis boy, 'money over bitches'?" He said to no one in particular. Then he studied the three faces that sat in the rear of the Excursion with him. The three young goons were at the top of the list. Six-Nine liked their swag. They were some good hand-to-hand fighters and had excellent chopper skills. Their ages ranged from sixteen to eighteen, their mouths were laced with platinum and diamonds, and they were dressed in Ralph Lauren Purple label suits. Six-Nine eyed each of them, one at a time, while sipping on his Promethazine and his Chateau-Paulet Cognac.

"If yawl don't remember nothing else in life, remember this. Everything a man do in life will always revolve around a bitch."

One of them removed a compact Heckler-N-Kach .40 cal and politely kissed the barrel. "This da only bitch I believe in, shawty."

Six-Nine nodded his head casually. *It's still a bitch, he thought.* Then he pulled on his Newport and exhaled a stream of smoke.

"Why you think niggas always name their weapons after bitches?" he asked.

They all had puzzled looks on their faces, trying to figure out the answer.

The Excursion came to a halt and the driver got out and opened the rear door. When Six-Nine stepped out into the parking lot, he thumped the butt of his cigarette nearly at the feet of the Dread.

The Dread cut his eyes down to the cigarette butt, then he thought about his position and caught himself. *Easy,* He told himself, and then he gave Six-Nine a humble grin. "Good evening, sir."

Six-Nine looked down at him. His stare was furious, and then he headed into the restaurant with nearly forty goons behind him. He was moving as if music was in his ears. The restaurant had a magnificent layout and the food smelled wonderful. As they were escorted through the front, Six-Nine looked around briefly at the many faces that were staring at them. "Do I look like mothafuckin' ET or something?" he asked the audience.

The maître d' continued on, escorting them to the back, where Hammer and his associates waited inside a nice secluded room with several tables of different shapes and sizes.

Hammer placed his eyes on Six-Nine and his so-called Cartel within a tenth of a second. Six-nine went directly toward his table with his henchman, Lil Willie right next to him. The remainder of the crew stood next to one another around the walls, dressed in suits, ties and gators.

Now they had Hammer's attention. He stood up with a scowl on his face. Before he uttered a word, the Governor tapped his hand, and Hammer leaned down to give him an ear. The Governor whispered, "Never hate your enemies. It'll play tricks on your judgment."

Hammer looked at the Governor and his eyes turned to slits. He thought about his words for a mere , and then he allowed a mask to cover his face. His eyes turned softer and more sympathetic. He extended his hand out to Six-Nine. "I see you brought company," Hammer said calmly.

Six-Nine held on to his hand, staring down his hawk-like nose. He made his eyes look vulnerable, nearly in pain. Then he said, "I'm just here to apologize to you for my actions. I really see dat I can't get money like I want to and be beefin' with one of the top officials in da' city."

Hammer continued to hold on to Six-Nine's hand and stared directly into his eyes. Hammer allowed his thumb to touch Six-Nine's middle finger, which Six-Nine didn't notice. He studied him, and thought of him as an opponent on the other side of the chessboard. That was a very clever move, and after the silence hung in the air, Hammer focused his attention on the shorter guy that stood next to Six-Nine.

He finally released Six-Nine's hand, and then shoved his hand in Lil' Willie's direction. "You must be Lil' Willie, the assassin."

Lil Willie shook his hand without a smile. "I'm just Lil' Willie."

Another stony silence, then out of the blue, a handsome and well groomed maître d' appeared, and four more followed. The back room could seat seventy-four, and the tables were set up in multiple configurations. They loaded the tables with Grace Family Vineyard wine, sautéed Wild Salmon with braised white beans, and Edward bacon. They brought out nearly forty 22oz loin lamb chops. There was steamed broccoli, grit fritters, hash browns and several other dishes to accompany the meats. Hammer had arranged for a special order of Bolivar Cigars. Razor sharp cigar snips were available also. One of which, he'd special ordered.

They all took a seat at the same table. Hammer sat across the table from Six-Nine. "I hear you a millionaire now."

Six-Nine rubbed his hands together. He couldn't hide his

excitement. "Too much money in da city for a young nigga like me not to be rich. And besides, I took your advice."

And what was that?" Hammer asked eagerly.

"Fools don't deserve no money."

Hammer nodded in approval, and then he looked at the Governor, who didn't say one word. This business was between only Hammer and Six-Nine. Hammer scanned the many faces in the room, until his eyes fell back upon Six Nine.

Almost everyone who had had some clout throughout the city had shown up for the meeting.

The maître reappeared with nearly thirty Steuben champagne glasses. Vincent tipped him about two hundred. He began popping bottles from table to table. Hammer then removed a velvet pouch that contained four Cohiba cigars. He took one for himself. The Governor got one, then Vincent, and last but not least, Six-Nine.

Hammer fired up his cigar first and calmly asked Six-Nine, "Do you understand the difference between kindness and weakness?"

Hammer exhaled a line of smoke. Champagne glasses were clinking at other tables, but not enough to interrupt their peace summit.

Six-Nine thought about the question briefly. Then he said in a joking tone, "With all due respect, everybody says that my elevator don't go to the top floor."

A smirk eased across Hammer's face when Six-Nine made his so-called, arrogant statement. Then he looked at his Dior wristwatch. Nearly forty minutes had passed. He needed to see where Six-Nine's heart was. He removed his custom made cigar snip from his pocket and placed it on the table before Six-Nine. "You wanna win me over?" Hammer asked in a low, raspy drawl. "My trust, my loyalty?"

Six-Nine's eyes turned into slits for a second while beaming in on Hammer. He slowly turned up his champagne glass and cut his eyes toward the Governor, and then to Vincent and Vincent Jr. When he looked back at Hammer, he shrugged. "Whatever it takes, pimp. I'm jus tryna' make the peace."

Hammer took another puff from his cigar. "Give me your fuck you finger on your right hand." He demanded in a non-threatening tone.

"Ease your finger in the circle of the cigar snip and press. Even a caveman can do it."

Six-Nine knew Hammer was joking; he had to be. He stared at him long and hard. The expression on Hammer's face never changed. "You takin' my kindness for weakness?" Six-Nine asked.

"With all due respect, everybody say my elevator don't go to the top floor."

"I know damn well it don't if you thank I'm bout to give you my finger."

"Sometimes, men of our caliber have to make sacrifices to continue to move forward." Hammer said calmly.

Six-Nine should've known. His eyes darted around the room to examine the rest of the faces, but nobody heard the conversation but the heads that were sitting at their table. His eyes went to the cigar snip, and they sat there for a minute. He leaned over toward his right hand and whispered in Lil Willie ear. "What you thank?"

Lil Willie whispered back, "Fuck all these niggas, pimp."

Out of anger, Six-Nine grabbed the snips, his heart pounding inside his chest while suppressing his anger toward Hammer, his eyes boring into his. Then he quickly turned on his game face, because he knew that Hammer would try to read him. He looked over at the Governor once more, and this time, the Governor was looking him square in the eyes. Six-Nine flashed a smile. *You'll be the first to die,* he said to himself. Six-Nine sat quietly for a minute, staring into space, lost in thought.

Around the room, gangsters were having fun. Champagne

glasses clinked together, and the smell of fresh garlic bread was in his nose. He glanced down at the table once more. His food was getting cold, his head and eyes went up toward the ceiling. A dimly lit chandelier hung directly above their table. He swallowed and lowered his head and eyes in one swift motion.

When he eased his middle finger in the circle of the cigar snip, he slid both of his hands underneath the table. He applied pressure, clenching his teeth together with force, and pressed the cigar snip again. Pain raced through his body, every inch, from his head to his toes.

When his finger hit the floor, blood poured everywhere. Six-Nine moved his chair out, reached down between his legs, and picked it up. He threw it on the table directly in front of Hammer and the Governor.

Hammer politely scooped it up and wrapped it in a linen handkerchief, as if it was a souvenir.

Six-Nine wrapped his hand in a couple of handkerchiefs and concealed the poison in his stare. Instead, he gave a defeated look. Sorrow and pain was in his eyes. He stood without warning and nodded to all the heads at the table.

"One more thing before you leave," Hammer said. "One of my associates by the name of Diamond..."

Six-Nine stared at Hammer once again; his blood was boiling through his veins. He definitely remembered Diamond, and he remembered like it was yesterday when he gunned down his wife at the Kroger on Cascade.

He nodded. "I remember." His voice cracked and his Adam's apple bobbed.

"So you know I know you were responsible for that incident." With that said, Hammer removed a shopping bag from the floor, pulled out a shoe box wrapped in a red ribbon and placed it on the table. "This is a gift from me to you."

Six-Nine became anxious. His eyes darted around and

finally rested on Lil Willie. After locking eyes with Lil Willie, he cut his eyes to the gift.

Reluctantly, Lil Willie removed the top from the box. He and Six Nine looked inside. There was a pair of Alligator shoes that looked very expensive and familiar. However, the worst part was that there were a pair of feet still inside the shoes that had been cut off at the ankles. Six-Nine squinted and took a deep breath. He knew whose shoes and feet they were, and that alone broke his heart.

"Even swap ain't no swindle." Hammer said and then paused. "Now we're even. No hard feelings, right?"

Lil Willie placed the top on the box and picked up their missing friend, LC's feet from the table.

"No hard feelings." Six-Nine finally said.

He turned and headed for the exit, with his Cartel behind him. Not one word was said.

4

Young Hollywood had Prime Minister status throughout the entire Georgia Prison System. His name rang bells at every camp. He was being congratulated on all levels, and his name was being mentioned in rap songs from artists all over Atlanta. Hammer even had radio and magazine interviews scheduled for him. And why wouldn't he? The clout was there for both of them, and it was steadily climbing. Young Hollywood had become a multi-millionaire, and that made the corrections officers flock to him as if he was God. However, he did great deeds for some officers, and helped several other prisoners. That alone made him feel greater than a King.

Today, he was laid out in his two-man prison cell, high on exotic sticky Kush marijuana, and reading an article on his favorite actress. She was half black and half Asian, with exotic eyes. The magazine layout had her posing on a rooftop terrace in New York, wearing mesh panties, a T-shirt, and six-inch Louboutins. She was in a reclining position on a chaise lounge, with her arms stretched over her shoulders. He smoldering expression, and the sexiness of the Manhattan skyline in the background made Young Hollywood's nature rise. He knew her favorite dishes, what she liked to do for fun, and some of her vacation spots.

Young Hollywood finally closed the magazine, and was quickly brought back to reality. He'd had several magazines, a few books, a couple of portable DVD players, and at least five personal cellphones. He kept the camp supplied with marijuana, cocaine, X-pills and meth. He had shampoo bottles stashed in other cells that were filled with Hennessy Black Exclusive, Remy Martin and three different kinds of white Vodka. All of this was indeed very small to him; he was strictly focused on his freedom. He'd made up in his mind that he wouldn't allow anything to stop him once his feet were on the ground. In his heart, he knew that day was coming soon. Even though the young go-getter possessed aggravated arrogance, he walked high with sheer confidence and major swagger. There were still a few people who wanted to be in his shoes, and even in his presence.

On the other hand, some hated him; didn't like his looks nor his conversation. He had his own motto for that, 'A sucker will never be prehistoric.'

A knock came from outside his cell door. He hurriedly tucked his phone underneath his pillow and stood up. At the door, he pushed the towel slightly to the side and stared at a short Mexican standing outside his door. Young Hollywood smiled. "Fuck you want, amigo?"

The Mexican spread his hands. "Come on, my friend." He yelled through the door.

Young Hollywood pressed the button. It clicked, then buzzed and he pushed it open. The Mexican was named Tequila, or at least that's what everybody called him around the camp. He was tatted up, covered with ink on his head, around his neck, and around his shoulders and chest.

Tequila entered and closed the door behind him. "We need Mota, my friend."

Young Hollywood folded his arms across his chest. He stood three inches taller than Tequila. There was a small grin on Young Hollywood's face, then Tequila said, "Let me look like you, my friend."

Young Hollywood laughed. "That will never happen, my friend."

"I'm handsome too." Tequila turned to the mirror. "A scar here, a bullet wound there." He pointed to his neck and face.

They laughed, then they dapped each other up. "You got cash money or your people goin' to Western Union?"

"Cash money." Tequila's eyes narrowed. He was the 'go to' guy for the Mexicans. His money was long, and he spoke very good English. Tequila bent slightly and used the front of his left boot to remove his right boot. He picked up the boot, then dug inside and removed a wad of newspaper. Inside the newspaper was seven crisp one hundred dollar bills. He handed the money to Young Hollywood.

He took the money and carefully fingered through it, then slowly cut his eyes back to Tequila. "Three ounces?"

"Fuck wit' me, my friend." He begin putting his boot back on.

Young Hollywood didn't respond, and they stared at each other for nearly a minute.

"Loyalty, my friend."

Young Hollywood finally cracked a smile and shook his head. "I'ma fuck witcha dis' time, mothafucka. You owe me."

Tequila smiled. "When I get deported, my friend, I'll be back to the United States. I'll come to Georgia. Whatever you need. Pounds. Kilos. Pills."

Young Hollywood walked toward the door. "Time will tell," he said as he left the room.

Noise was blazing everywhere, in the common area. Sports

on the TV, loud and boisterous conversations from the skin tables, and marijuana smoke filled the air. He moved across the floor, darted up the stairs, and ducked off into one of the cells on the top range. The room smelled like damp mildew, clothes, and sweaty socks. The two guys that were housed in the room were downstairs watching Lifetime, but they were on Young Hollywood's payroll as well.

He pulled the door closed and switched off the light. Quickly, he removed the dummy mirror and revealed a six inch circle hole that had been punched through the cinder blocks. He reached inside, grabbed one of the four state issued socks, and pulled it out. After he snapped the stainless steel plate back on the wall, he stuffed the socks down in his shorts and boxer briefs, and then left the room.

Back in his own cell, he removed the sock in front of the Mexican, pulled out four compressed ounces of popcorn mid marijuana, and dropped it in Tequila's hands. "Good business," was all Young Hollywood said.

He dapped up the Mexican and they departed.

5

———

Young Hollywood was stretched out on the gurney, surrounded by doctors and bright fluorescent lights. Tubes and wires ran from nearly every major vein in his body. He could smell the coppery blood odor creeping inside his nostrils, he'd been stabbed forty seven times and he was near death.

"Niggas finally got you too," a voice said.

Young Hollywood's eyes opened. A tube had been stuffed down his throat and the lights were blinding him. He squinted against the light and tried his best to see the face behind the voice. Shadows moved rapidly and fiercely around the room, blurred white figures on a mission.

"Scalpel." another voice said. "We're gonna have to cut him open."

Young Hollywood recognized the voice this time. To his left was Fat Man, standing in a white overcoat, a cigarette in one hand and an ax in the other.

"What da' fuck goin' on, shawty?" Young Hollywood asked.

Nobody answered.

From his peripheral vision he noticed the door open. Ghost

entered first in Kevlar chest armor over a hospital gown. He was filled with bullet holes. Scooter followed him in a wheel chair pushed by Hollywood.

Young Hollywood's eyes widened and he tried to sit up in bed, but the pain in his chest forced him back down.

Hollywood released the handles from the wheelchair and began moving toward Young Hollywood.

"Fuck these slimy ass niggas, pimp." He grabbed his hand, and then he added, "Being real is etched in your soul. And remember, real power can't be given. It must be taken."

Young Hollywood woke up, drenched with sweat. He got out of bed and got in a workout, and then he blew a personal joint of Purple Kush. Finally settled, he showered and watched ESPN while sipping on a huge cup of orange juice. By nine thirty, they were calling him to visitation.

His name buzzed through the intercom, but he didn't move. He was glued to the TV screen, watching the NBA greatest dunks in the last ten years. "Vince Carter, hands down," he said while standing in front of the TV.

———

Inside the visitation room, he met with his father, Hammer, Vincent and Kangoma. The three men were well dressed, in suits and expensive hard bottom shoes. Young Hollywood scanned their faces quickly. From years of dealing with cats in the streets and soaking up knowledge from books, he'd become obsessed reading facial and eye contact, mainly to detect any problems.

He knew Hammer and Kangoma very well. On the other hand, Vincent was another story, and he hadn't personally known him like that. Although Hammer had told him of his good deeds and that he was very loyal, to Young Hollywood, he'd had untrusting eyes. He was hiding something and he felt it in his heart. Before sitting, he hugged Hammer. They embraced for a brief moment. He gave Kangoma the same hug, a smile and they separated. When he got to Vincent, he only shook his hand and gave him a stare. He couldn't read his emotions, but he did feel something.

Vincent looked toward Hammer. He wanted answers, but he knew deep down in his heart that he wouldn't get them. At least not now anyway.

They all sat, nearly in unison. Young Hollywood was his own treacherous man, and he didn't care who knew it. Their circle sat in silence for a minute, Hammer was the head. The chief. The Boss. Don Status. He studied his son for a moment. He actually admired him, his demeanor and the energy that came from him. This was very important to Hammer. Just for this day only. When he cleared his throat, he carefully leaned forward, his elbows pressed on the table. He said to Young Hollywood, "A few days ago there was a meeting arranged."

Young Hollywood focused harder on Hammer.

Hammer went on. "Between myself, Six-Nine, Vincent right here and also Kangoma."

Young Hollywood's eyebrows bunched together and his eyes never left Hammer. He wanted to hear more, and Hammer went on.

"He proved his loyalty to me..."

Young Hollywood interrupted. "He could neva prove his loyalty to me nor you. Not until he's dead." He threw up his hand in mock surrender, and then he sat back and appeared to relax. "But if this is something that makes you feel comfortable..."

"I never said that I was comfortable, but this was something that had to be done. You should've seen it, a room full of killers packed in an expensive restaurant." Hammer grinned, then he stood and motioned for Young Hollywood to do the same.

He did, and everyone else held their place without one

word. Hammer walked over and threw his arm around his son's neck. They walked toward the line that waited for pictures. "I made that bitch chop off his middle finger." Hammer said.

Young Hollywood looked at him with a smirk. "Sho'nuff? You made him chop off his finger. Did you keep it?"

"Nah, but I did keep his homeboy's entire body except for his feet. I gave him LC's feet inside his gator shoes wrapped as a gift." They were inching up in line, slowly making their way to the cameraman. "Make me feel a little better, you know."

"You should've killed him right there in front of everybody. You won't get that chance no more."

They walked up on the small stage and posed for the camera side by side, both with serious facial expressions. The cameraman snapped four photos of them and they stepped down.

Young Hollywood paused and turned toward Hammer. "I don't trust dis nigga, Vincent." Young Hollywood said in a whisper.

Hammer clapped his son on his shoulder, then he embraced him and whispered, "You'll learn to."

6

As usual, Six-Nine was on to something, and he kept more than enough tricks up his long ass sleeves. There was always some kind of scam or either a flam running wild through his mind. It was early in the morning, and the beaming sun was beginning to force it's way through the expensive drapes that hung from his floor to ceiling window. His estate was huge, five bedrooms, four baths, flowing marble and custom furniture.

The exterior was constructed in smoke gray colored brick, with tinted windows everywhere. The lawn was green and perfectly manicured, with a brick driveway that curved into a circle where twin Lamborghinis sat.

The Atlanta Journal Constitution had already began to scar his name. The city was talking, and leaving rude comments and emails. One of the comments read, *I guess taking four human lives in Atlanta is the normal thing to do. Whatever happened to justice?*

Six-Nine was draped over a plush suede couch. One leg hung over the back, and the other one was stretched across the arm. After he allowed Hammer to take his finger, he went straight to the nearest hospital. He was sewn up and wrapped in less than two hours. His finger was still wrapped.

He finally sat up, both feet sinking into the Oriental rug. Across the room was one of his new soldiers who had proven his loyalty two days ago. This treacherous individual went by the nickname of Sabertooth because of the way his front teeth used to protrude before Six-Nine paid for him to have his entire front grill constructed. He didn't fit the description of a killer, or any type of goon for that matter. He had a simple look and smooth mahogany skin. The absence of facial hair gave him a baby faced innocent look. No tattoos, no gold teeth, and he wore wire-framed eyeglasses. The trick of the devil, basically.

Six-Nine stared at him while firing up a Newport. "When I look at you, shawty. I see a different future." He blew out a line of smoke and went on. "I'm tryna' do big shit around the city."

Sabertooth spoke in a soft and squeaky voice. "Like what?" he asked, then added, "An exclusive strip club? What about a sports car club?"

Six-Nine stood up from the couch, dressed only in linen sleepwear pants with a drawstring tied in a knot. He placed the cigarette between his lips, the smoke curled around his face. Six-Nine liked the way that Sabertooth spoke. He was trying to think like Hammer. What would he do in the future?

He smiled, then he asked Sabertooth, "Can you cook?"

"Cook what?"

"Food nigga. Real food."

Sabertooth grinned and flashed an even set of white teeth. He shrugged. "I can learn anything, pimp. They got culinary art schools.

Six-Nine stared at Sabertooth briefly. He drew on his cigarette again. "How long do you think something like that would take?"

"My homegirl took dat shit somewhere. I think it's called Blue something."

"Blue Flame?" Six-Nine asked grinning.

"Hell nawl, brah. I believe Cordon or something like dat. Shit might take at least eighteen months."

Six-Nine's mind was flipping again. The plan was sounding better and better to him. He'd had a vision that was out the roof. Culinary art school. It was very different. He would try something new that would give him more power. He flicked the ashes in a glass leaf ashtray. "This what I need you to go do. Find at least four young ladies. Ladies, not bitches. That mean choose them wisely. We want them to sign up for the school." He pointed his cigarette at Sabertooth. "You got to sign up with them. Yawl need cars and houses. Find 'em and consider it done."

Sabertooth nodded and stood. He dapped Six-Nine and they embraced briefly. He turned and exited the room, politely closing the thick oak wood door behind him.

When he left, Six-Nine grabbed a small black cordless phone and punched in a number. He moved over toward the fifteen-foot marble bar and poured himself a drink while waiting for someone to answer on the other end.

Finally, a soft female voice came through the phone. "Hello."

Six Nine downed a double shot of Patron Silver. He frowned slightly and said, "Wuss'up lil mama. Where you at?"

"At Grady." she shot back. "My lil sista is having her baby."

Six Nine frowned and snubbed his cigarette out; a concerned look crossed his face. "Your lil sister is only thirteen. You must got another sister that I don't know about."

"Yeah, dat one. You know she fast as hell."

Six Nine could only shake his head. News like that was sometimes disturbing. He finally whispered, "Any kind of way I can see you tonight?"

"I could, but I don't wanna leave her."

"It ain't dat important. Jus give me a call later on."

"Okay Boo. Love you."

Six Nine hung up and walked across the carpeted floor. He moved with a graceful swag as he climbed a carpet covered flight of spiral stairs that took him to the second level. He passed three doors, two on his left and one on his right, and entered the last room. It wasn't decorated as a bedroom, but more like an office with an exotic wood desk.

The furniture consisted of Ralph Lauren Home leather armchairs with brass nail heads, twin laptop computers, and two four-foot file cabinets were pressed in a corner.

He took a seat in one of the chairs and relaxed. A long stony silence settled over the entire house. He allowed his eyes to close, and he began to think about his now deceased partner, LC. He couldn't believe he was dead, moreover, he couldn't believe that Hammer had him killed and chopped him to pieces. L.C was a legend through the city, and several killers wanted answers.

7

A -Town Records and Studio was cramped with managers, producers and musicians from New York, LA, Miami, and of course, Atlanta. Local rappers and R&B singers were mingling amongst each other. Cuban cigars were handed out and trays of poured up champagne as well.

This particular room was set up like a huge den, with eight oak wood tables and eight leather cushioned chairs. More chairs and sofas were spread throughout the room. A few hired goons were using the two high quality billiard tables.

The entire front wall was made of glass, with a light honey colored tint. On the other side was an exclusive recording studio, lined with cherry oak paneling. In the soundproof room, two of Hammer's artists were recording a song. The beat was soothing and every head was bobbing. They were definitely hot, especially in the A, and of course, Hammer's arms reached all the way to Harlem and as far as Compton. He was trying to get in on every play like Ray Lewis. A new R&B singer could be in Dallas, Texas, or as far as Seattle, Washington. Hammer would hear about the artist and then send for them to come to Atlanta. On his expense, he would show them the world inside Atlanta, and then the next thing they know, they're signing on the dotted line.

His approach was similar with the rappers, except he'd show them the underworld in the city. Swag check them to another level. Turn me up, D.J. He could stuff twenty to thirty stacks into the pockets of unsigned artist on the strength and not miss it. He had done this more than once. Some of them went back to their own city and never returned. Others copped drugs with the money, went home to get it off, and never made it back. However, A-Town Records did have a nice roster that was getting longer and longer.

Inside his office, Hammer sat behind his desk, staring into the eyes of a young fierce hood cat who went by the name Quick. He had had a nice flow and a gift for arranging his words to make you listen at his music very closely. His eyes were filled with mixed emotions, energy and even more anger. The kid was indeed hungry, but Hammer didn't see it that way. He had drawn up a contract for Quick nearly eight months ago, and he had signed it then. Quick still hadn't completed two singles for a mixtape. That was a bad sign for an up and coming artist. Hammer didn't like dead weight. You lose revenue fuckin' with dead weight. That was his own famous quote to his managers, engineers, Co-CEOs and on down the chain. Now, Quick was sitting in a comfortable leather chair across from Hammer in a private office.

"Wuss'up, Hamma. Whatcha need to talk to me about?" Quick asked in a dry cracking voice.

For a minute, Hammer sat with his fingers pressed together, looking directly into Quick's eyes. Without saying a word, he removed two pieces of paper from a manila envelope and casually slid them across the desk to Quick.

Quick took the papers and read silently, with eyes darting back and forward, line for line. His lips moving, eyes right, then left, then back to the right again. For another minute or two, there was total silence in the huge headquarters office. When Quick looked up, he shrugged a little. "This my contract. What about it?" He was confused. In his mind, he was the best artist on the label. *This nigga must be miserable.* He thought.

Hammer drummed his fingers on the oak desk; the thumping sound was in rhythm. He did this for nearly five minutes without saying one word.

Quick was beginning to feel the pressure now. His stomach tumbled nervously to the point that he had gas. He'd heard a few rumors about Hammer, nothing to be too alarmed about though. At least that was how he had felt about the situation in the past.

The drumming stopped and Hammer allowed his eyes to turn cold and hard. He finally said, "I don't babysit no grown ass men." His voice was low and calm. He leaned toward the left side of his chair with his index finger pressed against the side of his face, his facial muscles relaxed. "Give me one good reason why I shouldn't tear up this contract right now."

Quick took a deep breath. "Hamma'... I'ma get it together, man." He stuttered nervously. His eye fixed on Hammer now. Then he added, "You know I can rap, I'm an entertainer."

"I never said you couldn't. I know you got a future, Quick. But right now you on some dumb shit, tryna go to every ass club and making it rain and all that shit. You got money to blow like that?"

"My people caked up like Betty Crocker. You know how dat shit be, Hamma. You from da streets too."

"What about the shooting incident last week in Buckhead? Your name was in it."

"Nigga disrespected my hoe, shawty... I mean, Hamma."

Hammer twisted his mouth in one corner. "Yo' hoe? So you mean to tell me you out here bout to catch a life sentence cause yo hoe. Which is probably nothing but a hoe anyway because that's what you address her as." Hammer paused. A sharp pain raced through his skull as if he'd been struck by lightning. He squeezed his eyes shut with an overwhelmingly ugly expression across his face. The palms of his hands pressed on each side of his head.

Alarmed, Quick jumped to his feet. "Hey brah, you alright?" He moved around the desk, and just as he made it around to Hammer, a sharp pain hit him. Hammer gritted his teeth, squeezed his eyes even tighter for a hot second, then he opened them and looked up at Quick with a frown.

Quick was standing over Hammer with one hand calmly on his shoulder. "How you feelin?" Quick asked.

Hammer shook his head quickly, trying to get his bearings. "What the fuck just happened?"

"I don't know. You must have caught a sharp pain. You closed your eyes and grabbed yo' head. Pimp you might need to go to the hospital."

There was a short pause.

Hammer slowly shook his head. "I'm good."

His head throbbed again, but not as bad as before. He pointed to a small refrigerator in the corner behind him. "Get me a bottled water."

Quick walked to the small fridge and retrieved the cold bottled water. He gave it to Hammer, and he rubbed the bottle across his forehead. That relaxed him. He twisted off the top and downed half the bottle. Then he removed a bottle of Tylenol 3 and popped two of them.

"Now look in the bathroom and wet me one of the face towels."

Quick did as he was told without one word. A moment later, he was back. "Man, you sho' you gon be alright?"

"Sit down." Hammer told Quick.

Quick went back around to his seat and sat down where they had started from the beginning. Hammer had the washcloth sitting on top of his head, nearly hanging over his eyes.

"Quick, you got to get your shit together." He paused. "It get lonely in them prison cells."

Quick listened.

"From this day forward, I'm gonna allow you to come stay with me. No hoes. No friends. No company. I want you to work with Mossburg."

Quick's eyes were intense. He wasn't even sure if he was hearing him correctly. "Let me get this straight. You gon' let me come stay with you at your crib?"

"At my estate. Just until you get your shit together." He paused and took another sip of water from his bottle. "Growth." he whispered.

8

E very day, for the next two weeks, Hammer and Quick went to the studio together. Faithfully. They ate together, along with Hammer's fiancé and little Corleone. The two chatted about everything from murder, to women and God. Quick looked at the situation as Hammer being his mentor. Hammer dropped knowledge on Quick as Socrates had given it to Plato, just in a more modern day fashion.

By the fourth week, Quick had stopped popping pills. After six weeks, he was off the exotic marijuana as well. He was in the studio even more faithfully now, sometimes up to fifteen hours straight. He'd come up with a hit single called "Naked", where he described the pure uncut bricks of cocaine that his people were touching. The song was gaining major radio play, and every club DJ in Atlanta was playing it. After two months, it caught fire up and down the east coast, and Hammer was ready to do the remix with Mossberg and the rest of the household name rappers in Atlanta.

Hammer came with the video, and Quick was on point. He began doing local concerts around the city and in Augusta. He was touring in Charlotte, North Carolina, and Greensboro, Alabama. His name was ringing all over. Two more months passed, and Hammer arranged for him to be featured on the cover of Don Diva magazine and an exclusive interview with XXL. Quick posed on the cover in a three-piece Armani suit and Mauri alligator skin boots. Instead of him looking at the camera, he was looking down at the image of the world beneath his feet. That was another one of Hammer's great ideas. He was becoming a marketing genius.

A few more days came and went. Hammer and two of his executive attorneys were sitting in his home office closing out a major deal when a knock at the door interrupted them. "Yes." Hammer shouted.

The door cracked open slightly, and then Corleone peeped inside.

"Gran'daddy. You busy?"

Hammer waved his grandson in and he came quickly, but not before closing the door behind him. He walked straight past the two attorneys and whispered in his grandfather's ear. "My daddy called."

Hammer nodded. He leaned down and whispered in Corleone's ear. "What did he say?"

Corleone was finding this amusing. A bright grin spread across his face, then he nearly stood on tip toe. He cupped both of his hands around Hammer's ear. "He told me to tell you that his people is coming home tomorrow."

Hammer kissed his grandson on his cheek and he gave him a nod of approval, but before he allowed Corleone to leave the office, he drew him close. "You see these two gentlemen right here?" Hammer pointed to both of the attorneys.

Corleone turned around between Hammer's legs and faced them. His eyes darting from one to the other. A few minutes ago, he hadn't even noticed them, and now he was examining them and studying their facial features, their hair and their clothing type. They watched him as well.

"These gentlemen here work for me. And if they work for me, they work for you as well. Go shake their hands and introduce yourself."

As a young gentleman, he did just that.

———

Later that day, Six Nine and Lil Willie were riding together in a gray service van. Lil Willie was behind the wheel and Six Nine rode in the passenger seat. He watched the scenery as they rode I-20 East. They got off in Covington Georgia, and nearly twenty minutes later, they were pulling into the winding driveway of an estate that sat one hundred yards away from the paved road. Six Nine sat up from his slouched position and looked out the window toward his left. His eyes caught the sight of a huge lake stretching behind the house. This was one of their hideouts that LC had bought before he was murdered.

After Lil Willie parked the van, they both stepped out onto the black asphalt flat top. The sun was out, and the sky was a crisp blue. Lil Willie took a deep breath, his eyes closed for a few seconds. "You smell that?"

Six Nine turned his nose and tilted his head back. He sniffed. "What is it that I'm supposed to be smellin'?" he asked.

"Fresh air, pimp. It's a different kind of living out here, this the type of atmosphere that'll give you a piece of mind."

"I can get a piece of mind in da city." Six Nine shot back, then he focused his attention on the house, and he was damn impressed. They hopped into a golf cart and took the trail that led them around back and across the green manicured lawn. They were heading down toward the huge lake that stretched at least four football fields on each side. There were at least ten houses surrounding the lake, and they all had docks.

Six Nine retrieved a pack of Newports and lit one. The smoke trailed away in the wind. When they got to the dock, there was an old man standing there in denim overalls, boots and a cigar hanging from his mouth. He waited by an eggshell colored motor boat.

"Who is Dad?" Six Nine asked, his eyebrows raised.

Lil Willie didn't respond. He parked the golf cart and stepped out. Six Nine paused briefly, wondering why Lil Willie hadn't answered him. They walked the length of the dock to where the old man was standing. Now Six Nine recognized the old man's face; he was black as crude oil and his hair was gray, short and nappy. His eyes were slits and blood shot red. Six Nine drew on his cigarette and his face turned into a smile. "Motha'fuckin, Blue," he shouted and thumped his cigarette butt in the water

Blue was an old gangsta from Atlanta who was in his mid-sixties. He'd ran with some of the best of them, survived hits and answered some as well. When the phrase, 'Old Money' was used, this was the man that they were talking about. And with the icing on the cake, he was also LC's uncle.

He extended his hand and Six Nine shook it, then Lil Willie did the same. The three of them got inside the boat, Blue behind the wheel. He started the engine, and within seconds, they were gliding across the water in a peaceful silence except for the engine of the boat. Nobody said a word, and ten minutes later, they pulled up to another dock that led them to another huge house that resembled a clubhouse at a ski resort.

There were two bigheaded Cane Corso Mastiffs that stood guard beside one another, as if they'd practiced that stance. Blue whistled from the dock and both of them sat down.

"I'm definitely feelin' this atmosphere out here, pimp." Six Nine said in a low even tone. He was rubbing his hands together and looking around as if he was a tourist who had just arrived in New York City. The sparkling lake danced like fresh cut diamonds underneath the sun, and huge pine trees stretched up toward the blue skies. This was a more than stunning view.

They moved up a steep hill and across a manicured lawn and scattered pine straw. When they got inside, Blue led them to an executive tailor made room that smelled like Brandy and stale cigar smoke.

Once again, Six Nine was amazed. He tapped Lil Willie. "Boss shit, shawty."

Lil Willie nodded in agreement. The ceilings were high, with oak beams stretching from one end to the other, and small pin lights were lined up in rows of three. Blue, Six-Nine and Lil Willie all took a seat around a square marbled table. Lil Willie picked up the latest edition of a Robb Report magazine from the table and began to casually flip through it.

Blue kicked off his shoes while staring deeply into Six Nine's eyes. He then folded his thick arms across his chest. "We all know that slippers do count," Blue said. Six Nine nodded and Lil Willie slowly lowered the magazine and fixed his eyes on Blue. He continued. "You can slip up and lose a young million dollars wit no problem."

"Another nigga can easily lose it, too." Six Nine said. His voice steady and calm.

Blue grinned, flashing a row of rubies and diamonds embedded in snow-white teeth. "Always... better them than you." His eyes went to Six Nine's hand. "What happened between you and Hammer?"

"Minor accident. Nothing major." was all he said.

"Yo business is yo business. However, somebody need to tell

me something about my nephew." The tone of Blue's voice raised a little.

Six Nine's eyes squinted slightly, but out of respect, he held his composure and refused to blow on the old timer. He took a deep breath and stared Blue in his eyes. "Hammer and his crew killed LC, is the word in the street."

"Is this a fact?" Blue asked calmly. His eyes fixed on Six Nine.

"His body ain't been found." Lil Willie said.

"So how do y'all know he's dead?"

The room fell silent. Blue eyes darted from Six Nine to Lil Willie. Neither of them responded. They didn't want to let him know that Hammer had given them his feet for insurance. "We really don't know for a fact," Six Nine said stubbornly.

Blue nodded casually, but he wasn't satisfied. He felt a numbness wash over his body. The lie that they had just told was devastating to him. Now he was battling with conflicting emotions. Blue was a vet though, and gangster down to the bone. However, he knew what he was dealing with before him. Six Nine was treacherous, and he would leave it at that.

Blue stood up and flashed a plastic grin that was fake as a three dollar bill. Six Nine caught his fake simile; that put him on defense. He stood up also and moved with swiftness. He felt like Blue was up to something, and he didn't want to get caught slipping, or down bad in other words.

Blue looked up at Six Nine. "Jus' relax soldier, everything good. I got some business I was working on with LC. Y'all can take a look at the project.'" He paused. "If you like it, it's another two or three million you can add to your stash. If you don't. You don't."

Six Nine looked at Lil Willie to get his thoughts. Lil Willie nodded in agreement. "It shouldn't hurt to listen," he said.

Blue looked back to Six Nine and spread his hands. "Five minutes is all I ask."

Six Nine nodded in agreement.

Blue turned and reached under his chair, removed a leather folder and handed it over to Six Nine.

Without hesitation, Six Nine took it and pulled out four sheets of paper and a small stack of photos that showed two kids on swing sets.

One photo was of a female; she had a petite model looking body and green eyes. She was the kids' mother. Another photo was of a tall handsome guy hailing from Chicago. He was a street nigga who wagged to the Feds. They call him Chi-Town da Don."

Six Nine was very interested now. "Where he located at?" He was staring hard at the photo.

"According to my sources, he's in Buckhead. He supposed to have a penthouse in a high-rise building."

"Well let's go get him." Six Nine said anxiously, the thirst was in his eyes.

Blue noticed this and filed it in his memory bank. He stared at Six Nine, but Six Nine was too busy gazing over the photos. Then Blue said, "The building that he supposed to be living in won't be completed until another six months." He paused. "At least the top floor anyway."

That was like a powerful blow straight to the mid-section of Six Nine's body.

"You got another address?" Lil Willie asked

Blue cleared his throat and moved around the love seat, all the time never taking his eyes off Six Nine and Lil Willie. He looked like a harmless and homeless peasant. But those that knew him, knew better. Blue cranked his finger. "Y'all follow me."

They followed Blue up four steps, to a short hallway lined with African art on each wall. At the end of the hall, there was only one door and it was thick and solid. Blue twisted the shiny brass handle and pushed it open. The room they entered had peach colored carpet on the floor. One wall was painted with flamingos and another was covered with seagulls flying over the ocean. The dome shaped ceiling made the room more than a home theater.

Blue directed them to a seat. He removed a large remote from a four-foot marble column. The remote dimmed the lights. He then directed it toward the projector screen as it was already half way emerging from the ceiling. When the screen found its final destination, Blue pressed another button.

The target appeared on the screen with his entire family exiting Lenox Mall. They were dressed like a millionaire family. Most made men didn't in this new age and era. Six Nine was very observant; his eyes squinted as he tried hard to focus on each picture that flashed across the wide screen. "This picture here was taken in Savannah Georgia at his favorite restaurant called the Bonna Bella Yacht Club," Blue said. "From my understanding, he has an estate here also, and another ranch home in Lagrange, Georgia."

"Why not in da city?" Lil Willie slowly asked. His eyes glued to the screen as well.

"That question has been asked and answered." Blue said as he wedged his fingers between each other.

Six Nine noticed his cocky tone, but held his tongue. He'd developed another genius idea. He was thinking about the Penthouse. Top floor. Six months. Then he said. "All I wanna know is can we get him?" A surge of energy was pumping through his veins.

The next picture was of a black Lexus GX 470 on the wide screen. The Chicago skyline was in the background.

"I got special orders not to harm this man nor his family. So that means that the job must be a burglary. No home invasions. No kidnappings."

"Special orders? Who he down wit', da motha fuckin' mafia?" Six Nine growled.

"Let's just say he's protected. We can touch him, but we can't touch him. All we want is the motha' fuckin paper."

Six Nine sat down, pulled out his pack of Newports and removed a cigarette from its pack. "You mind?" he said to Blue. Before Blue could respond, he fired up the cigarette.

Blue squinted and said, "Jus thump da ashes on da' floor."

Six Nine ignored him and began thinking long and hard about the lick that was being laid out on the table before him. *He can be touched, but he can't be touched.* He repeated the statement over and over in his head. He looked up at Blue. "What type of estimate figure we looking at?"

"I'm hearing at least fifteen million in cash."

"Split how many ways?" Six Nine asked as he pulled on his cigarette.

"Three." Blue said. He was eyeing Six Nine again, and he noticed how Lil Willie was staring at him.

"Two ways and you got a deal."

"No deal. It's a couple more hands in it."

Another long pause.

Six Nine drew on his cigarette again and squinted. The ashes hit the floor as he slowly shook his head. He looked Blue in the eye. "The Black Cartel is gonna have to decline on this one."

Lil Willie couldn't believe what he was hearing coming from the General's mouth.

"Shawty, we need this one. Five million will put us on top."

Six Nine gave Lil Willie a stare that would kill. He quickly turned his attention back to Blue. As he stood up, he extended his hand toward him. Blue took his hand and squeezed it. He looked up into his eyes with a mask hiding his real emotions. He wanted this lick just as bad as he knew they did.

"It's still good business, family. Maybe you'll change your mind in the near future."

Six Nine released his hand. "I usually go with my first mind, pimp." He stared down on the much shorter Blue to the point that it was intimidating. "Can we get that boat ride now?" When he left the theatre room, Lil Willie got up to follow.

Blue touched him on his shoulder. Lil Willie paused and looked at him. "Dude bad business," he whispered. Blue saw it in his eyes that he wanted in. "I know you want this lick. It's easy money."

Lil Willie placed a finger on his lips and gave Blue a slight nod. "Slippers count, pimp."

He left the room as well.

9

Their names were Apple Head and Muffin, and they were identical twin brothers that Young Hollywood had befriended while they were in prison. Both brothers stood six-three, with a powerful build. Strong arms and hands, barrel chest and wide shoulders. These boys were country strong with dark smooth skin and handsome features.

The twins were actually from Atlanta, but their mother had met a man named James Bradford when they were only five years old. James was from a small poverty stricken city in south Georgia called Albany. They lived there for the next eleven years of their lives before they caught their first murder charge. The twins were then sent to the Augusta Georgia Youth Development Center and released five years later.

The twins then returned to Albany with aggressive reputations for strong-armed robberies and kidnapping. People feared the twins, and they had every reason to do so. However, Young Hollywood had an eye for strength, loyalty and disciplined men of their caliber.

Today, they arrived at the Atlanta Greyhound Bus station, and no sooner than they exited the terminal, Hammer and

Kangoma were waiting for them in a glossy black Bentley. Hammer stepped out from the passenger side. Dressed in jeans and a cream colored linen shirt that waved on his body from the light wind, he spotted the twins standing across the street. He leaned against the Bentley and casually fired up a cigar.

"Hit the horn." he said to Kangoma.

From the inside of the Bentley, Kangoma pushed on the horn, and that even sounded expensive coming from the six-figure machine. Both of the twins turned their heads in the direction of the sound. Hammer's hand went in the air and he waved it side to side, gaining the twins attention. When they crossed the street, they shook Hammer's hand.

Hammer smiled to himself at the much younger brothers with such a powerful presence.

Kangoma stepped out from the driver seat, and without one word, he stood next to Hammer. He was his protector and didn't trust one living soul around him.

Hammer's eyes shifted from one brother to the other, and he examined them both within seconds. "Which one of you is Apple Head?" he asked.

The twin that stood to his right slightly tilted his head back and raised his index finger.

Hammer pulled on his cigar and the smoke streamed around his face. Without a word, he casually turned his attention to Muffin. "My son speaks highly of both of you. I hear that y'all two are interested in doing construction work."

They nodded their heads simultaneously; the definition of construction work in their field meant gun play and taking hits. Cleaning up messes and whatever else that was required for the young Goons to do. The twins were told to get in the rear, and Hammer and Kangoma got in the front. The four of them rode in luxury to the low sounds of Curtis Mayfield for the next thirty minutes, until they pulled up to a three bedroom brick home with a for sale sign sitting in the middle of the lawn.

They all exited the car and went through the side door that led them through the utility room and then inside the house.

The three bedroom house was spacious. There was a huge living room, kitchen and den. They went into the dining room where only a wooden square table sat with four chairs. "Have a seat." Hammer said while sitting down himself. Kangoma and the twins sat with him. "I'm sure my son has told you two about me."

They both nodded.

"Loyalty is first and foremost with me. That means if you got any distrust, any crossing me or anybody that I cosign for, you're in the wrong business with me. Your duty is to do what I need you to do, and my duty is to make sure you become wealthy and finically stable." He pointed at Kangoma. "This here is Kangoma, my African brother. He's the only person y'all will meet until Wood comes home. He'll train you two over the course of the next two months."

"Train us to do what?" Apple Head asked.

Kangoma then leaned in. "To side with your friends at all cost, even if they are wrong. I'll show you how to defend your dignity and give strangers a very warm welcome." Kangoma touched his temple. "We start here." Then he touched his heart. "Not here."

Hammer stood up and so did Kangoma. "This is where you two will be staying until further notice. I'll only give you one chance. No fuck ups. Period."

"Loyalty is a must. By any means necessary." The twins said in unison.

10

A tlanta to Vegas was a thought that constantly inhabited Six-Nine's head. He whispered it to himself over and over again, and the more he repeated it to himself, the better it sounded. He turned and faced a beautiful jet black female with a slim Coca-Cola bottle figure. She was slightly bowlegged, and naked to the bone, except for a pair of platinum Jimmy Choo heels.

The girl placed her hands on her hips and shifted her weight from one foot to the next. Her moves were graceful and elegant, far from an amateur. She was a seasoned veteran in the strip clubs all around the city, and had performed private shows up and down the entire east coast. Six Nine just adored the way she bounced her weave around, brushing it away from her eyes and face as if it was hers. Well at least it was sewn and not the cheap glue in weave. The thought of Atlanta-Vegas flashed through his head again. His eyes shifted to his missing finger, which was healed, but he still wore a band-aid over it anyway. He was gonna kill Hammer just for that. "Yeah pimp, you a dead motha'fucka." he whispered.

He grabbed a glass from the coffee table that was filled with Hawaiian Punch and promethazine codeine cough syrup. He took two deep gulps and began to bounce his shoulders and move side-to-side, as if the drink tasted so good, he had to hit the Bankhead Bounce.

The stripper looked at him with a smirk, then she moved toward him in a cat-like manner. Six Nine took her hand and pulled her down to his thigh.

She sat down and he glided his finger down the side of her face. "You are a cool ass nigga, you know that?"

"Some say different," he said. "Stand up."

She stood with no hesitation and he did as well; he was feeling himself now. Six-Nine towered over the girl.

She looked up at him as they stood in the center of the hotel room floor and grabbed his hand with the missing finger. As she casually massaged it, she aksed, "What happened to your finger?"

He sipped from his glass and swayed in a light two step dance. "I lost a bet with the Falcons." He responded nonchalantly.

She twisted her lips. "I'm serious."

"Me too, Vick let me down again." A playful grin spread across his lips. Then he made his eyes cross.

"You're a real comedian, you know that right?"

They laughed and stared into each other's eyes. He finally said, "You a pretty cool chick. A nigga like me could kick it witcha on some long term shit."

They stood there for another moment or two, moving as if music was playing. Six-Nine guided her into the bedroom, where a comfortable king sized bed hogged up the majority of the bedroom. Six-Nine sat at the foot of the bed and the girl stood between his legs. He sucked on her nipple and kissed her stomach. "You fuck with the pills, baby?" He asked her, then he sipped from his glass again and sat it on the floor.

His hands traced the curves of her ass cheeks as she wrapped her hands around his neck. Then she said, "I do, but only the Blue Dolphins."

"All the freaks like the Dolphins." He dug in the front pocket of his jeans and pulled out a small Ziploc bag filled with colorful X-pills.

The girl's eyes widened with excitement. She fell to her knees instantly and began massaging his penis through his jeans. She then unfastened his pants and pulled the zipper down.

Six-Nine picked through the bag and found her two pills. One Dolphin and a yellow one with a Tweety Bird stamp. She opened her mouth, and he gave her both of them. She pulled his hard throbbing penis out, and without using her hands, she worked her tongue and lips around the head of his penis. Allowing her mouth to fill with saliva, she deep throated him without gagging and popped him out her mouth like a blow pop. She held his penis as if she was speaking into a microphone.

"Before we get started, I want you to put one in my ass for me." She kissed the tip of his penis, then twirled her tongue around it. Her glistening eyes looked up at Six-Nine. "Pretty please."

He began singing a verse from one of Rick James' old songs.

"She's a very freaky girl. The kind you don't take home to mothaaa. She will never let yo spirits down... Once you get her off the streets."

She wagged her head from side to side, still serving him like the Don. Six-Nine fingered her with two fingers, and then without warning, he stuffed another Blue Dolphin in her anus.

Her eyes closed for a brief moment, and then batted once more. She went into beast mode, slapping herself in the face with his long hard penis. He stretched his long legs out and leaned backwards, his glistening eyes were on her now.

"If you can cook like you give head, I'll keep you."

She paused for a moment, still holding his penis. Her stare was serious as if she really cared. She knew how to play her role to this made man who was about to take over the entire city of Atlanta. She carefully lifted Six-Nine's hand up to her lips and politely kissed the bandaged finger.

Six-Nine remained cool and continued to enjoy the luxurious head. But in his mind, he was still thinking about Atlanta-Vegas, his own business plan. The more he thought about it, the closer he could envision it coming into existence. *Anything could work,* he said to himself. *Anything, and anybody can get it. Anybody.*

———

The following morning, Six-Nine was in a deep sleep next to the flawless black stripper when he got a call on his cell phone from Lil Willie. He picked up on the fourth ring and answered in a groggy tone. "What it do, pimp?"

"Good news."

"I'm listening."

We just hit the lick on that nigga Chi-Town Da' Don."

Six-Nine shook himself wide awake. This wasn't supposed to happen, but now that it did, he needed to hear the outcome. "How much?"

"Seventeen," he said, and then added, "but we got bad news too."

"I'm listening."

"The whole family."

Six Nine closed his eyes and rubbed his hand across his forehead. He hung up the phone without another word. They'd killed the entire family, and it was only supposed to be a burglary. He couldn't do anything but lay there, mind spinning in circles. And all he could think about was how Lil Willie went against his last word.

BOOK 2

YOUNG HOLLYWOOD

11

ONE YEAR LATER

Young Hollywood was called up front for a special visit from one of his attorneys. When he got to the multipurpose room, it was buzzing with activity. Counselors were signing papers and teaching classes such as, Thinking for Change and Moral Recognition Therapy. Young Hollywood dapped up a few associates and gang members that he knew. There were two cert team officers standing guard outside of the small office. They were there to keep an eye on him, due to the fact that he had a strong reputation for manipulating nearly anybody that stepped in his path. His eyes met them both before he stepped into the small office.

When he stepped inside, his attorney was standing up facing him from the other side of the desk. He was clad in a three-piece gray pin-stripe suit, and wore his hair in a tight and clean oiled ponytail. He was one of the high profile slick talkers from Manhattan. He extended his hand out to Young Hollywood. "Mr. Terry Keys." He gripped his hand. "How's it going?"

They shook hands and held each other's stare. "Under the circumstances..." Young Hollywood turned up his lip as if he was an Italian mob boss. "I'm good. What about yourself?"

"I'm excellent, and I'll be doing much better once we get you out of here." He smiled and opened his personal leather briefcase and sat down behind the desk.

"Sound bout right." Young Hollywood rubbed his hands together.

"As of now, we'll be going back to Fulton County on a motion for a new trial. We got everything arranged where you'll sit up there until after the holidays. The Judges are always in good spirits after Christmas and New Years. We'll ask for an appeal bond and they'll grant it."

"So next summer, I'll be on the streets is what you're trying to tell me?"

"By the grace of God, you'll be on the streets by spring break. Furthermore, your father has promised me a golf course if I can spring you by then.

"He usually keeps his word."

"And when you are home, we'll have a couple of relaxing games of golf on my course, of course." He smiled.

Young Hollywood allowed a smile to spread across his face. He leaned up in his chair. "I'ma hold you to your word."

The attorney stood. "Mr. Keys, you've hired the second best Jewish attorney in the United States."

Young Hollywood stood. "Well maybe I should've hired number one."

The attorney grinned and extended his hand. "Of course you did. It's my father, and he only deals with your father. I guess you can say we're all the best of the best." On one final shake, the attorney said, 'See you next week in Fulton County.

———

Back inside the dorm, Young Hollywood went into his two man cell. His bunkmate was sitting at the desk reading a hardcover novel titled, *What's Going On* by Nathan McCall. He looked up from the book and stared at Young Hollywood. "What it do, brah?" He asked, then turned toward him and closed the book. "People talkin' good or what?"

Young Hollywood sat down at the foot of the bottom bunk and took off his all white Air Force Ones. He looked at his bunkmate. "I won't speak too fast, pimp," he said. "But everything is in motion."

"Man, come on wit' all the indirect talkin'. Let me know what's up."

Young Hollywood grinned and stood up. He stripped himself of his blue and white state issued stripes and stepped into a pair of Nylon gray Jordan shorts and a wife beater. He looked at his bunkmate again. He could've explained everything to him detail for detail, but he wasn't the type of person that Young Hollywood wanted to share everything with.

Young Hollywood went inside his wall locker and removed a rolled blunt of some exotic marijuana that he'd wrapped in sandwich wrap. He looked at this bunkmate again. "Where yo' lighter?" He carefully eased the rolled blunt to the corner of his mouth.

His bunkmate stood from the desk and reached in the far corner of the top bunk. A knock sounded at the door and they both turned toward it. Young Hollywood quickly removed the blunt from his mouth and cuffed it. Outside his door was a guy by the name of Black Saddam. He looked directly into young Hollywood's eyes.

"Let me in, nigga," he said from outside the door.

Young Hollywood pressed the button and the door came open.

Black Saddam entered the room wearing a black Kufi and standing six feet tall. He extended his hand. "Attorney visits, that's a blessing brother." He said and locked hands with Young Hollywood. They clapped each other's back.

Young Hollywood smiled and nodded, then the blunt reappeared in the corner of his mouth. "Close the door." he told Black Saddam. He looked to his bunkmate, and before he could say anything, he handed over the lighter. Young Hollywood lit the blunt and looked back at his associate then back to his bunkmate. "Let me speak with my people for a minute."

"Can I hit the blunt first?"

Young Hollywood shook his head, reached in his pocket, pulled out a much smaller joint, and banded it to his bunkmate.

He eased out the room without a word.

When he left, Black Saddam could only shake his head. "Soft ass nigga couldn't say thank you." He sat on the desk facing Young Hollywood.

Young Hollywood passed the blunt and said, "It's all part of the game." He closed his eyes and allowed a line of smoke to ease from his mouth. "Suckers will never be prehistoric, I say."

A silence set in between the two of them, and then Black Saddam asked.

"How the lawyer talkin'?"

Another short silence. "I'm outta here in a few months. I should be back on Rice Street by next week."

Black Saddam pulled on the blunt again. He looked at it and blew the smoke onto the fire. He looked up at Young Hollywood. "You ain't coming back either, is you?"

"I don't plan on it." Young Hollywood dapped his associate up.

"Don't worry, lil brah. I gotcha."

12

T he law firm in Buckhead was built nearly fifty years ago. The outside was made of gray stone and large glass sheets. On the inside, it was equipped with armed guards, glass elevators, high tech surveillance, weight rooms, steam rooms and two huge dining rooms with marble laced fireplaces.

Inside the huge conference room, there were five well-dressed men sitting around a shiny mahogany conference table. Coffee was poured up and passed around amongst the elite heads. One of the men at the table was a managing partner at the firm. His name was John Barker. His friends called him J.B. Next to him was his father-in-law, and also one of the Fulton County Judges named William Peterson. William Peterson was the active Judge who would handle Terry Keys' motion for a new trail. Next to him was his father. Their names were Author Mason and Author Mason Jr. The next man was a private investigator who had done research on the entire case from head to toe.

They sat around for nearly two hours going over the errors that were discovered in the case. They spoke about the witnesses who had testified, and even the co-defendant. In the Judge's eyes, the case was very bizarre and disturbing. No one on the face of this earth could point a finger at Young Hollywood nor put him at the scene of the crime.

Author Mason Sr. spread his hands. "It's basically an open and shut case," he said. "There are at least fifteen reversible errors in this case with strong loopholes."

"Give up this one, Mr. Peterson." Author Mason Jr. said. He winked his eye at him and sipped his steaming cup of coffee. "Your Christmas bonus will be a promising six figure check," he added.

John Barker smiled and looked at his father-in-law. "The pigeons are lined on the rooftops." Indicating that everybody has to eat, including the pigeons.

"A ballpark figure?" the Judge asked the Masons.

"Let me hear your ticket. Something reasonable."

The Judge shrugged nonchalantly, then he looked toward his son-in-law and back at the Masons. "Let's say a quarter million."

The Judge removed his reading glasses and casually braced himself for a rude outburst.

Instead, Author Mason Sr. pulled out his cell phone and punched in Hammer's number.

"Hello." Hammer answered from the other end.

"Mr. Hayes, good morning. This is Author, how's it going?"

"I'm good, how about yourself."

"Excellent, can't complain. Listen, can you add a charity bonus check for a quarter million to your Christmas list?"

"Will my son be home for Christmas dinner?"

Author Mason dropped the phone and covered it with his hands. His eyes went straight to William Peterson. "Can he be home before Christmas?"

The Judge leaned over toward John Baker and they whispered to one another for a few seconds, then the Judge gave a smile and a nod of approval. "It's a deal."

Author Mason smiled and brought the phone back up to his face.

"Mr. Hayes."

"Yes."

"We have a deal."

"Good business then. I'm waiting on you."

"I'll give you a call in a bit. Thank you." He hung up.

———————

It was three days before Christmas when Young Hollywood walked out the front door of the Fulton County courthouse. It was cold, and the North Georgia air made him shiver. Hammer stood in the parking lot in a full-length mink, and Corleone was next to him outside a double stretch Lincoln limousine. When he approached his father, there was a wide smile across his face as they embraced. Corleone joined in and they all hugged in one big happy circle.

Hammer clapped his back and whispered in his ear, "Glad to see you."

"I'm glad to see you, too." He looked down at his son, leaned down, and picked him up. Corleone held him tight around his neck and they moved toward the rear door of the limousine.

Kangoma got out, moved around to the rear door, and opened it. He hugged Young Hollywood also before entering the limousine. Loyalty was written all over his face.

Corleone entered the limo and then Young Hollywood, followed by Hammer. Kangoma closed the door and quickly moved back around to the driver seat.

Tuxedo Park Estates was just north of downtown Atlanta. A world-renowned neighborhood, it was filled with corporate executives, athletes and celebrities with unparalleled privacy and tranquility. The majority of these homes sat on large wooded lots or either private park style landscaping. The limousine crept through this affluent community and eased down Tuxedo Court. They pulled up to a unique baby mansion, rode through an electric gate, and moved up the concrete winding driveway.

Young Hollywood stared from the rear window in amazement. He looked at Hammer. "This is top of the line," he said. "How much you paid for this?"

"The ticket was three point five million," Hammer said. "But I didn't pay for it. You did."

"If I paid three point five million, I'm ready to sell this motha'fucka."

"Ohh Daddy, you can't say no curse words. My teacher at school says it's bad for your soul and your food wont digest properly."

Young Hollywood looked at his son as the limousine came to a halt in front of the house. "She may be right." He looked to Hammer. "So you trying to tell me I own this?"

The rear limousine door came open and before Hammer stepped out. The only thing he said was, "Basically."

Corleone followed Hammer, and then Young Hollywood stepped out, stared around the house, and allowed his eyes to scan the entire neighborhood. Corleone raced toward the front door and Hammer gave Kangoma the signal to go ahead inside. When he left, Hammer faced his son.

"We pulled it off."

Young Hollywood smiled. As he stared at Hammer, he noticed that his eyes were tearing up. They hugged again and held each other. "This will be the first and last time you'll see me shed a tear."

Young Hollywood held him tighter. "I love you, man."

He whispered in his ear, "You better." They parted and Hammer looked him over. He put his hand on his shoulder. "Let me tell you something, as a man, and as a father."

Young Hollywood knew this was something more serious. His eyes beamed into Hammer's as he braced himself.

"How do you feel about Sasha?"

"The truth? I feel she betrayed me to the utmost."

There was a long silence between them. Young Hollywood swallowed and waited for his father's response.

"Corleone needs his mother in his life. And before I just made a move, I wanted to hear from you about how you feel about the situation." Hammer nodded toward the house. "She's inside now. Besides your grandmother, Sasha is the only female that I trust with him. With that said, we got other important issues to handle. Let's go inside and take a look at your new mansion."

13

Inside the mansion, Hammer removed his mink at the door. The house was warm, high ceilings and very spacious. Young Hollywood was amazed. He moved to the middle of the living room floor, which was laced with white and gold veined marble tile. With a sigh, he flopped down on a brown double stuffed leather couch and rubbed his hands across the suede. He kicked his shoes off and stood up again. The Oriental rug felt like heaven under his feet as he walked across the room to where a huge fireplace was burning real wood logs. He stood there for a minute, lost in thought, with his hands extended as if he was warming them.

Hammer was behind him, watching him think. He sat down in a leather chair to the right of Young Hollywood and allowed him to enjoy this peace of mind. Then without warning, a voice disturbed his moment of silence. "Daddy." Corleone yelled.

Young Hollywood spun around and searched for his son's voice. He looked up and saw him standing at the top of the stairs. He lost focus when he saw Sasha standing up there next to him. She was flawless, he had to admit. His eyes were locked into hers and they stared at one another for nearly a minute.

Then she took Corleone's hand and they began walking down the stairs.

He tingled on the inside; he wasn't expecting this. Not her, not his first day home anyway. When they reached the bottom of the stairs, he noticed that she was even more beautiful. Her hair was dyed a light honey blonde, and cut short and cute. She was casually dressed in a white silk blouse and black slacks that hugged her hips. Her Coach perfume was soft, and it intoxicated him as he got closer.

Hammer stood up. "Corleone."

Corleone looked at his grandfather with a questioning expression on his face.

"Let's go shopping," Hammer said.

Corleone dropped Sasha's hand and said, "I'm ready."

"I'll see y'all later on," Hammer said to Young Hollywood and Sasha.

Young Hollywood stared at him briefly and watched him and Corleone fade from his sight.

"Well, do I at least get a hug?" Sasha moved toward him before he could respond. She wedged her arms underneath his and he wrapped his arms around her. Her scent was intoxicating to the point where he was on her neck and nibbling at the three-carat diamond that hung from her earlobe. "I won't ask for much." She whispered in his ear as she ran her hands underneath his shirt. She kissed his lips slowly, and then pulled away from him and looked him dead in the eyes. "All I wanna do is live. I'm dedicated to you and our son only." Fear was in her eyes as a tear rolled down her cheek.

Young Hollywood could feel her hands trembling against his chest and he quickly pulled her closer by grabbing the small of her back. He brushed the tears away from her eyes. "You've straightened your face, Sasha. Meaning you've proven your loyalty to me. We were kids when we met, and we're grown now." His tongue slipped inside her mouth and she relaxed in his arms, her eyes closed. He could feel her heart pounding inside her chest.

———————

Inside the shower, not only was the water flowing, but they were surrounded by black marble. Young Hollywood sucked on Sasha's nipples. Her head was back, and her nails were in his back as they were caught up in the moment. He finally entered her tight vagina. She wrapped her arms around his neck and nibbled on his earlobe.

"Fuck me," she begged.

He went deeper and her eyes stretched wider. He could feel the stinging pain from her nails clawing across his back.

He went even deeper, then he eased out and plunged harder again. "You like that?" he asked her.

Her alluring eyes were nearly closed now, and her breathing was heavy. Sasha's body was moving in rhythm. Young Hollywood picked her up. His thick hard penis was in her stomach as he walked her toward the bedroom. He carefully laid her at the foot of the bed, her legs spread open. Young Hollywood laid on top of her soft elegant body as her tight vagina seemed to open and close around his penis.

"Dick so goooood," she moaned. She grabbed his ass cheeks and made him grind deeper.

An hour later, Young Hollywood was coming for the second time and Sasha was on three. He got up and went into the shower, and within fifteen minutes, he was walking around in a dark terry cloth Burberry robe and suede slippers. Inside the huge bedroom, he looked around in amazement. There was an eighty-inch flat screen TV on the wall. He grabbed the remote and turned it to ESPN.

Sasha came from the bathroom wrapped in a warm

comfortable robe also. Her hair was wrapped in a towel. "You want me to cook you something to eat?" she asked.

She moved toward him and rubbed her hand across his wavy hair.

With the remote in hand, he stood to his feet and kissed her softly on her cheek. "Nothing heavy, maybe a sandwich or something."

She grabbed his hand. "Come to the kitchen with me."

He followed Sasha into the kitchen area. It was spacious, with stainless steel appliances and marble topped island and counters. Young Hollywood grabbed a bright red apple and bit into it. The sweet juices burst inside his mouth. "So what kind of business you got lined up for yourself?" he asked her.

Sasha opened the refrigerator, removed sliced tomatoes, a head of lettuce and a pack of smoked turkey breast, and took it all to the counter top. She looked over at him as he stared at her, waiting for an answer. "I'm into real estate at the moment, and I'm taking online business in pursuit of my Master's Degree."

"So just a real estate agent?" He bit into the apple again.

"Oh no, boo." She smiled. "I have my own... Well, we have our own company under your father's corporation."

"What about the bonding company I've been hearing about?"

"From my understanding, all of the paperwork is in place. He has a building, but he's been waiting on you to come home." She pulled out four slices of wheat bread and carefully laid them on a wooden chopping board.

"No mayonnaise," he said, and then he walked toward the glass window that overlooked the large backyard. He stared out, lost in thought. A million and one things were on his mind, and he knew that he would now have a heavy responsibility on his shoulders. Nothing he couldn't handle, though.

Sasha walked up behind him and massaged his shoulders

and neck. He tensed, but then he relaxed. He turned and faced her. "I guess it's my turn," was all he said.

This time, a smile was on his face. He wrapped his hands around her waist and pulled her closer, he gripped her soft bottom again as she untied his belt and opened his robe. When she gripped his penis, it was already growing in her hand. Sasha fell to her knees before him and stared up at him before kissing the head of his penis. She eased him inside her mouth then slowly brought him out, then deep again.

A loud horn blew outside. Without hesitation, Sasha stood up and tied Young Hollywood's robe. She turned and walked back toward the bathroom. "The sandwiches are on the counter." She said as he left the kitchen.

Young Hollywood walked over to the counter, grabbed one of the turkey sandwiches, and bit into it. Then he heard Corleone's voice.

"Where you at, Daddy?"

"I'm in the kitchen."

Corleone walked in, followed by Hammer. He looked Young Hollywood up and down and gave him an approving look. He hugged him again. "How you feel?"

"I'm good."

They parted and Corleone took off running to another part of the house.

Hammer and Young Hollywood walked out to the all glass sunroom and sat down across from each other. Hammer looked him square in his eyes and said, "First of all, we are not in competition with dudes in the streets. Don't get me wrong, I know you gonna do you, but our major focus is the music business."

Hammer spread his arms out evenly and said, "That's our foundation." He paused, eyes dead serious. Then he added, "Any illegal activities one month strong then we'll rest for six to eight months." He paused again. Then he went on. "This nigga,

Six-Nine, is strong in the streets. I gave my word around the city and even to my mentor that our beef was squashed as long as I'm in position. After the first of the year, you'll be in position, and I want him dead. No if ands or buts."

Young Hollywood smiled. "That's what I'm here for."

14

The next day, Young Hollywood and Hammer, accompanied by Kangoma rode out to the Governor's mansion in a Maybach with the smooth sound of Sade playing through the car. When they pulled up in the circular driveway in front of the house, there was an Aston Martin sitting in front with a rear flat tire.

Kangoma looked in his rearview at Hammer and Young Hollywood. He was glad to see the father and son connection. It was like an overwhelming glow that Hammer possessed. He looked more at ease now. Similar to a cancer patient finding out that he is in remission.

Hammer caught his stare from the mirror. He bowed his head slightly at Kangoma and then he opened his door. Young Hollywood opened his door also and both of them stepped out at the same time, casually dressed and exuding sleek gangster-ism. They moved up toward the front door, and before they could ring the bell, someone opened it from the inside. It was the Governor. He looked worn down and drained when he answered.

Young Hollywood was staring at him and having flashbacks

from when he was thirteen years old and he had met the Governor for the first time with his big homeboy, Hollywood.

The Governor examined Young Hollywood up and down and realized that he had that still coldness in his eyes. He looked to Hammer and they grinned at each other.

"Yawl come on in."

"You ain't went broke have you, J.W.?" Hammer said in a joking manner. Then he added, "I thought you had a maid to answer your door and shit like that."

Young Hollywood looked at Hammer as if he couldn't believe that somebody would insult the Governor as he did. The Governor paused and slowly turned to face Hammer. "If you would've got here earlier..." he said before he burst out laughing.

Hammer laughed also, and with that said, Young Hollywood realized that the two of them joked with each other that way. His eyes darted from his father to the Governor and he even allowed a small smile to play across his lips. They went through another set of French doors, and then through the kitchen and inside a spacious sitting room with suede leather sofas and love seats bunched round a huge stone-encased fireplace. There was a huge nine foot tall white Christmas tree in one corner with boxes of gifts underneath it.

"Make yourself at home." The Governor said.

Hammer walked over to the Christmas tree and picked up one of the boxes. The name label read: Erica. He shook the box and held it to his ear.

"Put folks shit down," The Governor said from across the room.

"You didn't get me nothing for Christmas?" Hammer asked as he searched under the tree.

The Governor ignored Hammer and turned his attention toward Young Hollywood. He extended his hand and Young

Hollywood gripped it firmly. "I'm glad you could make it home with us this Christmas. How you doing?"

"I'm good." Young Hollywood said. "What about yourself?"

"I'm blessed."

Hammer walked over, took a seat in an ash-colored suede chair, and crossed his legs. The joking was over and now he wanted to listen. The Governor eyed Young Hollywood and leveled his arm and hand about four feet from the ground. "The last time I seen you, you was this big," he said. "A man trapped in a boy's body." He paused briefly but he never took his eyes away from him. "Do you remember the last conversation you and I had together?"

Young Hollywood nodded slowly, his eyes fixed dead into his. "You asked me did I know how to play Monopoly. And I told you that I was the best, and then we talked about the only way I could lose is when everybody team up against me."

"Some things you just don't forget." The Governor said. He rubbed his hand across his salt n pepper beard and looked at Hammer. "Cognac, no ice." He was joking, but he wanted that drink for real.

Hammer stood and left the room, the door closed behind him.

The Governor looked back at Young Hollywood. "It was Christmas night of nineteen ninety one when you came out with Hollywood, and I shared with you about knowledge and wisdom. I told you that in order to be a good leader, you had to be a damn good follower and an experienced listener."

Young Hollywood nodded. "I remember that. You also said that the great men in this world wasn't born great and you have to grow and earn your greatness."

The Governor nodded slowly.

Hammer came back into the room with an expensive bottle of Cognac and three glasses. He gave his son a glass and then handed the Governor his. He half-filled everyone's glass and set the bottle on the table.

The Governor held up his glass, and Hammer and Young Hollywood touched glasses with his. The clinking sound rang through the air and vibrated off the walls. "You home now, your foundation is built on solid ground. We are one team. Not a one-man team. You get where I'm coming from?"

Young Hollywood nodded, then he sipped the Cognac from his glass.

Hammer was listening closely as well, because he knew the Governor had more game and knowledge than the average scholar or professor, and that's one of the main reasons that he brought Young Hollywood to see him.

"And most importantly, everybody is trying to eat off of somebody. It's a lot of strong teams here in Atlanta. Niggas coming from everywhere and they wanna eat. However, we were born and raised here. My name been holding weight since the seventies. Yo' daddy name been holding the same amount of weight. He's knocked off damn near every slimy mothafucka from East Atlanta to the Westside. Now at the same token, the younger generation is on some other planet shit. Take this nigga Six-Nine for example. Young, fierce and heartless. I don't trust him and neither does your father. He got a strong team, they eating good in the streets." He paused and sipped his drink. The warm Cognac eased down his throat as he glanced at Hammer.

He gave him a nod as if to tell him to go ahead.

The Governor went on. "What good does it do to make the playoffs and get knocked out in the first round? Better yet, why go the Super bowl if you're not prepared to win the championship?"

Then Hammer said, "You want a ring, don't cha?"

Young Hollywood looked at his daddy. "Damn right."

"Do your name hold weight as being an A-Town Veteran?"

Young Hollywood smiled. "If it don't... It will."

The Governor touched his temple. "You move easy. You out thinking a lot of the suckers out here these days. Good judgment and swiftness is just a few keys to success. But Six-Nine has to be deleted like a text message."

This time, Young Hollywood held up his glass, and Hammer and the Governor toasted with him. "Terry Keys is back."

Then the Governor said coldly, "Your adversaries is a must."

15

On Christmas Eve, Young Hollywood rode in the passenger side of a smoke gray Phantom while Kangoma drove. It was mid-day, nearly three o'clock PM, and the streets of Atlanta were flooded. The first stop they'd made was at his old project, Hollywood Court. Kangoma cruised the Phantom through, and Young Hollywood scanned the scene. Kids were playing in the cold, and young hustlers were huddled in different groups. Young Hollywood squinted when he noticed an older guy whose face he recognized from several years back. He was dressed in black leather pants, a white quarter cut mink, and white Jimmy Choo dress shoes. Diamonds sparkled from underneath his dreads, and he was posted in front of a Porsche Cheyenne SUV.

When Young Hollywood pulled up in front of him, he stepped out from the passenger side while Kangoma waited and watched from the driver seat. Young Hollywood walked up to the guy with the dreads and they made eye contact to assure that they knew each other. The guy stared at Young Hollywood from head to toe, and didn't know him from a can of paint.

The stranger looked calmly at him and asked, "Wuss good, pimp? You must be the Feds."

Young Hollywood froze, but still allowed a smile to play across his face despite the low blow comment that he'd just received. He extended a balled fist and introduced himself. "I'm Young Hollywood."

The guy with the dreads looked at him much harder now, collecting old names and faces from his memory bank. "You and Scooter fell on the murder charge on dat nigga, Ghost?" He asked, more confident now.

Young Hollywood nodded. The tension was easing now. "Yeah, Hollywood, Bone, Fat Man..."

The dread was sure he remembered Young Hollywood. "You killed dat nigga Kangol Black at the Summit back in the days."

"They said it was me." He shrugged and added, "But I didn't do it."

"Well, the streets said you did it."

"The streets got a mouth." Young Hollywood said, then he basically switched the channels. He asked the stranger. "Lil Fred and Peter Boy still out here?"

"They mama still out here. Them niggas been missing since last summer."

That was a devastating blow for Young Hollywood.

A Cadillac EXT rolled up, it was black with tinted windows. The thunderous bass vibrated the project windows. The guy with the dreads began bobbing his head. This was his crew that had pulled up. The driver side window fell, and a cute yellow female with a Santa Claus hat on was driving. Young Hollywood looked at her. Her eyes were on him for a minute.

She gave him a seductive look and looked at the dread. "Wuss Gucci, baby?" She opened the door and stepped down in fitting jeans and high heel leather boots with a suede turtleneck. She sashayed to the dread and hugged him. "Black Cartel baby."

"Black Cartel." The guy said back to her. He kissed each of her cheeks and when she departed from him, she pointed at Young Hollywood. "Black Cartel?"

"I'm Hollywood, baby."

She seemed impressed and extended her manicured hand out to him. He politely extended his own hand to shake hers, but instead she turned it for Young Hollywood to kiss it.

"I decline." he said.

Kangoma stepped out and raised his head above the roof of the Phantom. "Sir, we must leave."

Young Hollywood looked back at him and noticed a look in his eyes that said that it was time to go. Without another word, Young Hollywood walked a couple of feet to the passenger side door. Before he got inside, he looked back at the dread head and gave him a small salute with a slight head bow. The dread did the same thing. A salute followed by a bow of the head.

Young Hollywood got in the passenger seat of the Phantom. Before Kangoma could pull off, the girl in the Santa Claus hat walked up to the passenger side window and stood there. She was waiting for Young Hollywood to roll his window down. Instead, he saluted her also, then they pulled off.

Easing the Phantom on through the horseshoe shaped street, there were several kids pointing at their car, and some of them rode close beside them just to look inside.

Young Hollywood glanced over at Kangoma. "Thangs ain't like it used to be."

Kangoma glanced at him briefly, then his eyes went to each of the rearview mirrors. "Time waits for no one," he said, "and changes everything."

Briefly, they rode in a stony silence. Young Hollywood scanned the streets. His old stomping ground. They rode up Simpson and made a couple more stops. In the course of forty five minutes, they'd gone through the Bluff, Summer Hill and Allen Temple. Young Hollywood spoke with a couple of old comrades that he knew from prison and before he'd been locked up back in the nineties.

Now he was realizing that Six Nine had the streets nearly on lock with his infamous Black Cartel crew. At least seventy five percent of the streets anyway, and that had definitely made him curious. Relaxing on the passenger side of the Phantom, he could see his reflection through the crystal clear glass, and without hesitation, he asked Kangoma, "Would it be possible to bring some African child soldiers here to Atlanta?"

"It's possible. A few strings would have to be pulled, and I definitely highly recommend it."

Young Hollywood nodded slowly while staring at Kangoma. They exchanged looks for a moment while paused at a red light. "I won't just waste all my time trying to hunt Six Nine," Young Hollywood said. "I wanna hit him with the element of surprise."

"I understand exactly where you coming from." Kangoma said.

The light turned green. He pressed the gas pedal and moved with the flowing traffic.

16

The gates opened automatically. They were twelve feet high and made of solid iron. This was only the entrance. When they separated, the movement was slow. Surveillance cameras were mounted to trees and hidden in bushes. They moved freely, and high powered lenses zoomed in on a pair of twin aqua blue Aston Martins that followed closely behind one another.

More expensive cars filled with guests began to creep through the gates and up the asphalt top driveway. Four shiny black Maybachs with heavily tinted windows came next. *This was either the mafia or some of the Black Cartel crew.* A coat attendant thought as she watched from the security booth.

On the inside of the twenty-two thousand square foot, three level estate that sat on nearly twenty-five acres of land in Alpharetta Georgia, Lil Willie sat comfortably inside a rather large oval shaped Jacuzzi, his head tilted back resting on the edge. He had his eyes closed, but he was far from sleep. *Just allowing my rich mind to wander,* was something he had started saying since he'd scored on the lick several months ago on the dude, Chi-Town the Don.

The jets underneath the water massaged his body and made him feel comfortable. Lil Willie was a genius in his own right. He'd organized bank jobs and several successful home invasions, and he was second in command in the Black Cartel. A straight certified Goon.

"Baby," a soft voice whispered in his ear. It was the Spanish chick he'd imported to the United States. She spoke broken English and worshipped the ground he walked on. "All... guest... here now." She eased closer, kissed his cheek, then the ten-carat yellow diamond that sparkled in his left earlobe.

Lil Willie never opened his eyes, nor did he turn to face her. Her exotic perfume wafted underneath his nose. That triggered him for a minute. He was sharp though, and held onto his composure. Without warning, he said, "Hand me my phone."

She retrieved his cellphone and quickly punched in his baby sister's number.

She answered immediately. "Hey boo." She chirped happily.

"You should've been here an hour ago," he said, sounding a little agitated.

Little Willie was always concerned about his baby sister; she was most important to him, and he held her close to his heart. Just recently, he'd bought her a club of her own downtown called the ACES. It was highly exclusive and polished, better than any other club in Atlanta. "I'm leaving out now. I'll be there no later than forty minutes."

"Sound bout right. Don't be speeding, you know how them folks is during Christmas time."

She blew him a kiss through the phone. "I love you, boo. See you in a few."

He ended his call and handed his girl the phone. Lil Willie then pushed himself up out the water. Suds covered his chest, waist, and public hairs as well. He stepped out onto the cold marble tile, walked into a huge shower, and quickly rinsed off.

The Spanish girl was standing outside the shower glass with a thick Burberry beach towel. She was a sight herself, standing five nine barefoot. Her skin was bronze and smooth; she had the nicest ass and hips a man would want to see, and a set of firm breasts and hard nipples. Lil Willie had paid for her to have implants and ass injections, this was what he wanted.

Her icy blue eyes were untrusting, and she only wore a sky blue thong.

When Lil Willie stepped out of the shower, she politely gave him the towel. Their eyes met briefly, and then hers fell down to his soft hanging penis. She watched him dry off, and looked back into his eyes. Something was going on between the two of them. Lil Willie couldn't care less though, it was Christmas night, he was a millionaire, and he didn't give damn about nothing. Sure enough no bitch. *You mad? Stay mad.* He said to himself.

Lil Willie knew she wanted some wood. He simply didn't feel like it, and shook his head no. The girl yelled out angrily in Spanish. She ignored his rejection and went to him anyway. Taking his soft penis in her hand, she politely kissed the head of it.

He laughed to himself and brushed her away. Then he walked across the wide marble floor and went into his walk-in closet. There were several shelves, and each one was lined with something different. Over forty pairs of alligator skin shoes and boots, everything was hand crafted. It was even rumored that he'd gone to Florida and hand-picked his own alligators from the Everglades, paid to have them skinned and dyed, and then shipped to Atlanta.

There was a display of tailor made suits, tuxedos and linen. Several different color minks and leathers. His watch collection and jewelry was unheard of. Lil Willie moved further into the closet toward a cherry oak dresser drawer. He removed a pair of silk boxers and slipped into them. Then he yelled out something in Spanish. One of the few words he knew, anyway.

His girl appeared in the doorway of the closet, holding a blue Kevlar vest. Not the big bulky one, but the small light weight one that would fit neatly underneath a thick T-shirt. Lil Willie stared at her nakedness. She was indeed gorgeous, and damn near flawless.

His eyes danced all over her. He finally said, "Come here."

She dropped the vest on the floor next to where she was standing, and then she gathered up her long jet-black hair and spun around on the ball of her heels. On her back was a detailed dragon tattoo in green ink, and the eyes of the dragon were ocean blue like her own.

He turned his back and strapped on a simple looking watch. However, in street value, it was worth two kilos of cocaine. Drought season prices.

She said something else to him and he tried to hold his smile. He turned and faced her. They gave each other yet another cold penetrating stare.

He finally nodded.

She fell to her knees and hands, and began crawling slowly toward him, with movements like a leopard stalking its prey.

Lil Willie checked his watch. He needed to be downstairs where the action was. "Hurry up," he said. "You better not get one drop on me or the floor."

She smiled and wrapped her lips around his penis.

17

D ownstairs on the first floor inside the elegant great room, which was decorated with huge chandeliers and white ivory drapes, Six-Nine circulated through a sea of beautiful women who were dressed in expensive Marc Jacobs dresses. Some wore backless Donna Karen, and strapless Dolce & Gabbana with matching heels. They were in Cartier diamonds, all different colors.

These were top notch grade A women. Some slim and petite, and some had the most curvaceous bodies a man would want to see. A piece of pussy out of this house tonight could cost anywhere from ten grand, on up to a quarter million dollar estate. Ain't tricking if you got it, though.

Six-Nine was in a Gucci suit and matching shoes. His neck and wrist were foolish, covered with heavy platinum and sparkling diamonds.

Standing at nearly six feet eight inches, he towered over nearly everyone. From behind his lavender tinted Cartier glasses, he noticed that there were a lot of eyes on him, as if he was about to make a speech. His face was impassive as he held his long stem champagne glass in the air. He signaled one lady, and she got to him moments later. She had the same features as the Spanish girl upstairs. They were sisters, a year apart, and both of them were under Six-Nine and Lil Willie's spell. He pulled her closer and whispered something fancy in her ear.

She left just as fast as she came.

Six-Nine checked his watch like he was waiting for a grand appearance. Maybe he was. He always kept some kind of trick up his sleeve. His metal navigation system was on now, cocaine was draining in his throat and he was rolling good on X-pills.

He moved outside to a glassed in patio and pool, where major hustlers mingled. Major dope boys from coast to coast were in attendance. Six Nine noticed a couple of NBA players to the far right, entertaining several women. He gave them a nod and that was it. He shook hands with local rappers from Atlanta, and a couple gangsters from Memphis; some of them he recognized and some of them he didn't. However, Six Nine didn't care about any of them. *These mothafuckas is here to show me respect.*

He checked his watch again. Another ten minutes had passed, and Lil Willie still hadn't come downstairs. He passed more guests, took a glass of Patron on ice from a passing waiter. He downed it and spoke to a couple friends.

Several naked females were having a volleyball game in the swimming pool. Music bumped through the loud speakers and everyone was having a good time. Six-Nine killed the remainder of his champagne and set the glass down on a table filled with model chicks who were in the last issue of the XXL magazine. He took an available seat next to a tall dark skinned chick with almond shaped eyes. Without a word, Six Nine removed her left breast from her dress and began sucking on her nipple.

At first, she was in shock and froze, and then her eyes moved around the table at the rest of the females and the look that they were giving. *It's okay,* they seemed to say.

Then, out of nowhere, a guy approached in a suit and
bowtie looking like a straight nerd. His name was Sabertooth.
He tapped Six-Nine on his shoulder, and then leaned down and
whispered in his ear. "The Christmas gift has arrived," was all
he said.

"Damn," he whispered.

He tucked the girl's breast back inside her dress, stood up,
and followed Sabertooth through a patio door and around the
side of the house. Two minutes later, they were moving across
the green manicured lawn. Motion lights came on as they
headed down the wide asphalt driveway, which was lined with
several stretch limousines, and some of the most expensive cars
in the world. The closer they got to the entrance gates, the more
curious Six Nine became.

His heartbeat sped up when he saw Lil Willie running
around in small circles. No sound came from the street, where
the small circle of people stood. Six Nine was taking long
strides now, and finally, he arrived where everyone had their
weapons drawn. He pulled up next to Lil Willie, who was
kneeling down in front of a casket that had just been dropped
off with a big red ribbon on it. The picture was overwhelmingly
gruesome.

Six-Nine looked at the mutilated body. It was only the head
and both arms, the face was still pretty as if it was just made up.

Lil Willie didn't move, he couldn't. Something had a hold of
him. "My baby sister," he finally managed to whisper until he
couldn't control himself. His heart felt like it was being ripped
from his chest.

Six-Nine grabbed him and held him. He looked down at Lil
Willie, whose face was streaming with tears. "Calm down," he
whispered. "Too many guests inside, lets cancel the party."

Lil Willie broke down and buried his head in Six Nine's
chest. Six Nine looked at Sabertooth while he held onto Lil

Willie like a baby. "Get the casket out the street." He then whispered in Lil Willie's ear. "Let's go inside and talk."

When Six-Nine and Lil Willie got upstairs, they went to a private room that was set up like an office. Eight surveillance monitors were lined up next to one another, and on the small TV screen, they could see everything going on in the rest of the house. People were still partying as if nothing had happened. Six-Nine removed his jacket and stared at Lil Willie, who was sitting on a leather sofa with his hands covering his face.

"Who you think did this, pimp?" Six-Nine asked.

Lil Willie looked up, his eyes red and deadly. His hands begin to tremble nervously. He stood quickly and stared up into Six Nine's eyes. "It was Hammer," he said in a positive tone.

Six Nine slowly shook his head. His arms folded across his chest and his eyes bored dead into Lil Willie.

Lil Willie felt that something wasn't right. He asked, "You don't think it was Hammer?" Lil Willie's face held a question now. His eyebrows bunched together and he spread his hands. "Who was it, then?"

The worst thing Six Nine could've done was flash a small grin.

Lil Willie pulled out a glock quicker than John Wayne on a western. He aimed it at Six Nine's chest and took two steps backwards. "You had something to do with this."

"Nah, brah. Chicago niggas." Six-Nine said calmly. "You know they found Blue night befo' last, dropped off at his mama house the same way. As far as me, you know loyalty is everything to me."

They heard a quick knock at the door, and then Sabertooth entered. His eyes searched the room. Lil Willie had dropped his glock down to the side of his right thigh, out of Sabertooth's eyesight. He closed the door behind him and said evenly, "I know who did it."

Lil Willie's eyes stretched wide open and he walked up to Sabertooth.

Sabertooth pulled out a note with bloodstains on it. He handed it to Lil Willie.

Not thinking, he tucked his glock back inside his waist. When he unfolded the letter, Sabertooth side stepped him, wrapped his arm around Lil Willie's neck, and locked on him with the other one. His struggle was useless, and within seconds, Six Nine had removed his glock from his waist. He was gagging for air and his eyes were begging for help.

"Number one rule, never cross me. I declined on that lick, and you went against my word and pulled it off anyway." He cut his eyes at Sabertooth.

"Give him some air." He looked back at Lil Willie. "You know how I play. I need your stash, simple as that. And I'ma make sure you and your funky ass sister rest in pieces together."

Lil Willie collapsed in Sabertooth's arms. Six Nine's eyes went to Sabertooth and a small grin appeared across his face. "Slippers count, pimp."

18

Over a month had passed since Young Hollywood first came home. It was February 2003, and Young Hollywood and Kangoma had been in North West Province, South Africa, for two weeks. They were staying in an exclusive luxurious hotel, one of the best in the world, for that matter.

The Palace at Sun City is secluded in the Pilanesberg Mountains. The air has a mysterious scent, nothing you'd smell in Atlanta or the United States for that matter.

An atmosphere definitely fit for a King, and that's exactly what Young Hollywood thought himself to be. He had his own suite, and inside the suite, the walls were covered in maple paneling with plush carpet running wall-to-wall. There were two bedrooms with overstuffed king sized beds.

This was a new learning experience for Young Hollywood, having never left America before now. He'd only left Atlanta once outside of his prison bid, and that's when he went to Vegas. Today, he was out on the balcony with a beautiful view of the jungle. Kangoma was sitting across from him, and they were eating rice and delicious roasted goat meat. Kangoma drank boiled milk, while Young Hollywood sipped on a Coca Cola with crushed ice.

Young Hollywood stared at Kangoma. "Brah, I wouldn't have thought in a million years that I'd be in Africa." He ate a fork full of rice then added, "and then we here in this palace, I damn sho' didn't think y'all had no shit like this over here."

"This is a rich country, Hollywood."

"Not what they show on TV, all the starving kids and shit. They don't never show no shit like this."

Kangoma sat silently for a minute, and then he stood and looked out over the balcony. He closed his eyes and took a long deep breath, and then whispered, "Never take life for granted, there's only two choices. You either win or you lose. If you're a thinker, it automatically puts you up on your adversaries."

Young Hollywood sipped his Coke. "And when it's duck season, the guns must go... BOOM!" He used his hands as if he was shooting a gun. There was another short silence between the two of them. Then Young Hollywood asked, "So what time ya people suppose to get here?"

"Maybe night fall or early in the morning. Until then, we'll relax. We'll go down to the Lost City golf course."

———

On the golf course, Young Hollywood and Kangoma rode around in an elegant Cadillac golf cart sipping on drinks from the Tusk Bar. The sun was blazing, and the atmosphere was breathtaking, featuring palm trees and beautiful women. This was definitely where the rich people hung out. They took practice shots and just rode around and enjoyed themselves. An hour later, Kangoma got a call from the head general of the Tutsi Militia in Uganda. That call was then transferred to another man named Zwayile. Thirty more minutes passed, and

Kangoma received another call from Okelo, an accountant in East Africa. Okelo worked for Kangoma, and transferred a lot of money through offshore accounts from the islands to Africa to the United States.

"Five hundred thousand has been transferred into their account. When you receive your product, you give me a call and I'll transfer the other half a million."

"Thank you," Kangoma said and hung up the phone.

The following morning, Kangoma received a call from the lobby. He went downstairs, along with Young Hollywood, where they met an African man who looked rough by his face and hair. His eyes were yellowish looking, and he was dressed in a two-piece cocaine white suit and white crocodile shoes. His teeth were snow white and very striking, although he never flashed a smile or offered a handshake. He slightly nodded, turned, and began walking toward the lobby doors.

Kangoma and Young Hollywood followed him outside. The morning air was fresh, and it exhilarated both of them. The African in the white suit led them to a Mercedes SUV and opened the rear door, where four nappy headed teenagers sat at attention. They were dressed in rag clothing. Two of them wore Khaki pants, dirty tee shirts, and worn down boots. The other two were in cut off denim pants and fatigue jackets.

Kangoma looked them over and pulled the African in the white suit to the side. "You can't bring them in here dressed like this."

"Zwayile sent them, how they dress is out of my hands. Yo' business now," The African growled.

"Let me go to the plaza and grab something for them to wear," he said to Kangoma.

Young Hollywood went to the backseat of the SUV and opened the rear door. "What size shoes y'all wear?"

The four young Africans looked at Young Hollywood. The first one closest to him spoke with a French accent. "Seven."

The one next to him shrugged. "Maybe seven, too."

The other two responded, eight and nine.

Young Hollywood sized them up with his eyes on their shirt and pants sizes. He went inside the hotel, and twenty minutes later, he came back with four shopping bags and gave each of them one. "Y'all change into this, and when you're dressed, come on out."

They all nodded in agreement and their faces brightened instantly. Young Hollywood walked over to where Kangoma and the African in the white suit stood. "These li'l niggas bout to get fresh," he said.

No more than three minutes had passed before the rear door swung open, and the first young man stepped out. He was dressed in a colorful soccer jersey with the imprints of the South African flag, black cargo shorts with white Nike Soccer cleats on his feet.

Young Hollywood nodded in approval and Kangoma did the same, then the other three filed out of the SUV one behind the other. They were dressed in the same color soccer jersey, black shorts and white Nike cleats. They looked like a small four man soccer team.

"Now that's more like it." Young Hollywood said, eyes directly on them. He could see into their cold-hearted souls when he looked them in their eyes.

They stood without a word, and acted as if the clothes didn't even matter.

Kangoma looked at the African in the white suit. "We need the paperwork on them."

The African in the suit walked around to the driver side and hopped in. Kangoma jumped into the passenger seat and closed the door behind him.

Young Hollywood looked down at the youngest boy and asked, "Y'all hungry?"

Without a word, they all nodded.

Then Young Hollywood asked, "All y'all speak English?"

Again, their heads nodded, and then one of them asked, "Is this your palace?" He turned and looked up and around at the huge hotel.

Young Hollywood laughed. "Nah, I wish it was, though. Cause this some playa shit."

"Playa shit?" Another one questioned in his deep French accent. "What is that?"

Young Hollywood threw both his hands in the air as Kangoma stepped down from the Benz SUV with a leather briefcase. The African in the white suit rolled the passenger side window down and yelled out something to the young Africans. They all looked up and saluted the driver, holding their hands at their forehead until he pulled off. They removed their hands from their forehead and quickly fell out of line and turned to face Kangoma and Young Hollywood.

Upstairs in the King Suite, Young Hollywood and Kangoma went over their paperwork, including their birth certificates and social security numbers, passports and all legal documents to get them back into the United States. Nearly three hours had passed, and they had all showered and ate. Now they were sitting at a marble top table that sat all six of them comfortably. Kangoma looked over their paperwork again; this time, he was examining their resume, their trained skills with assault rifles and handguns.

Nzile was the youngest, at thirteen years old. The darkest one next to him was named Biko. He was fourteen, and a highly trained killer since the age of ten. Biko's choice of weapon was the machete and the sword. Kimani was also fourteen; he was the tallest of the four and had a caramel complexion. His eyes were opaque and very cold, another frontline guerilla who didn't have a heart or any emotions. Last, but not least, was the shortest one and also the oldest. His name was Moyo and he was fifteen years old. According to the paperwork, he was forced to kill his own family, then another family that witnessed it. He took pride in decapitating heads, and was even caught playing Soccer with an enemy's head while on a mission.

Young Hollywood read over the paperwork also, and he was satisfied. He rubbed his hands together. "Y'all ready to go to Atlanta?"

The youngest, Nzile, looked at Young Hollywood. His oval shaped eyes were bright. Then he said in French accent, "All the players play... far wide... Afro and braids... Gangsta' ride."

Young Hollywood was amazed. The young African was singing Outkast, right before his eyes. He looked at Kangoma. "He already ready for the city."

19

W hen Six-Nine and Sabertooth pulled into the parking lot of club Aces, all eyes were on them. They stepped out of the cocaine white Lamborghini and left the doors up, stuntin' hard for the crowd. This was Six Nine's club now, and he didn't care what nobody had to say. So what it was rumored that he'd had lil' Willie killed for the Chicago boys? And he damn sure didn't care that LC was gone, especially after what Blue had told him. He was ready to make his circle much smaller. Paranoia wouldn't let him trust like he wanted to.

The two bouncers at the door guided them in; one removed the velvet rope. Females gazed in their direction. "Six." One of them shouted in a sexy tone. As usual, he threw up the deuces in her direction and never looked her way. When they got inside the club, he slipped on his platinum frame tinted Cartier glasses.

Sabertooth admired Six Nine and wanted to be just like him. They snaked their way through the crowd and the bouncer led them directly to a private room that was decorated with expensive suede furniture, thick carpet, and a beautiful female sitting behind an oak desk doing paperwork. She looked up when they walked in, and flashed a smile as she stapled a stack of papers and handed them to Six Nine. She handed another stack over to Sabertooth.

They both sat down and started to read. The music from the club vibrated the walls, but that didn't disturb them. As they quietly read, the girl stood up, moved around to the front of the desk, and leaned against it with her feet crossed.

She addressed Six Nine. "This is the blueprint for Atlanta-Vegas, you won't be able to buy this property around the club right here. But the property that's on this paperwork is in Cobb county—"

"It's got to be in Fulton County," he interrupted her. "Anywhere else will be a catastrophe."

The girl looked up at him with her mouth twisted in one corner, as if she couldn't believe what Six Nine was saying. Then she said, "Apparently, you don't know my father. He designed and built two of the biggest country clubs in Atlanta, and the Judge House and sub division in Cobb County. Out there, with his stamp of approval on the construction site, you can get away with murder."

Six Nine and Sabertooth exchanged half grins. Six Nine looked back at the girl. "What do you think about the idea and the project?"

"A foreign sports car club with a private membership. You must have a foreign sports car to be a member. It sounds good, but I still can't grasp the full concept."

Six Nine sat down on the couch to her right. He motioned for her to join him.

She walked over and sat down on the couch next to him. Six Nine threw his arm around her neck. He looked at Sabertooth with a slight nod, telling him to leave the room. He stepped out, and Six Nine looked at the girl from behind his tinted Cartier shades. "Let me know if you can see my vision." He kissed her on the cheek, her eyes staring into his.

He removed her breast from her blouse and bra and began playing with her nipples until they started to swell and harden.

She took a deep breath. "You don't even know my name," she whispered.

"When I first seen you, I said to myself, she look like she got some good pussy." He sucked on her nipples harder. Then he added, "Good Pussy is my personal name for you. That was earlier today. On your business card, it says Erica Daniels."

Erica was surprised; most guys from the streets didn't remember names, just faces and bodies. She blushed. Her eyes closed for a second or two and she nibbled on the corner of her lip. "So what makes you think that we're about to fuck?"

"The Blue Dolphins make me think that I can fuck any broad I want to. But since I'm not rollin' tonight, I don't think we're about to fuck."

He kissed her lips and then he stood up in front of her.

She grabbed his bulging penis through his pants. "Ecstasy pills are not good for you," she whispered while unzipping his pants.

"Did da FDA tell you that shit?" He asked jokingly. A grin formed on his lips; by then, she'd freed his half hard penis.

She looked up at him with a smile, and then she examined his penis underneath and on the sides. "You need to do stand-up comedy."

"I will, if you ever get me up." He laughed at his own joke and removed a pack of Newports from his pockets and a lighter. By the time he fired up his cigarette, she had had him in her mouth.

"Now you've grasped the entire concept," he said with a sort laugh.

Erica cut her eyes up at him as she deep throated half of his penis and slowly pulled back. "You got my pussy wet as fuck."

Six Nine pulled on his cigarette while Erica spit on his penis like she was trying to put out a fire. She quickly sucked it up.

"Well, you better control yourself, young lady. I don't fuck on the first date."

"It's after twelve. We met yesterday."

He pulled his cigarette again. "I knew y'all corporate bitches were freaks."

20

Young Hollywood had been back from Africa for almost a month. The first thing that he and Hammer did was hire a private tutor for Nzile, Bika, Kimani and Moyo. Their teacher would get them familiar with American customs, teach them better English, and allow them to recognize and know their position. Kangoma would enhance their skills and abilities on the streets in Atlanta. And on top of that, he'd teach them patience and serenity, and moreover, the value of life itself.

Today, Kangoma had the four of them dressed in Polo shirts, jeans and Jordan tennis shoes. Their hair was cut neatly and their fingernails were clean. "Respect all women here, unless I say otherwise." Kangoma said to the four of them as he sat at the head of a marble table in his home.

Their meal was Bobotie, which was a South African dish, similar to meatloaf, only with raisins and baked eggs. It was served with yellow rice, coconut, and banana slices, and they drank Tropicana orange juice.

"What did I say, Nzile?"

Nzile looked up at Kangoma. "Respect all women, unless you say otherwise."

Kangoma nodded, his eyes darting around the table. He paused at Moyo. Their eyes stared into each other. Kangoma nearly knew their strengths and their weaknesses. Which one had quick tempers, and who thought fast on their feet. He figured that Moyo needed counseling more than the other three.

"No Biltong?" Kimani asked with his eyes fixed on Kangoma.

Kangoma shook his head and casually stuffed a forkful of yellow rice into his mouth. He chewed slowly and then swallowed.

"Biko, what would you do if the police ever caught you at the scene of the crime?"

"Silence at all cost."

Kangoma nodded. "Correct."

Moyo looked at Kangoma. "We shouldn't kill the police?"

"Correct." Kangoma said, then he added, "Silence at all cost. That's all that matters." He touched his chest. "Allow me to do the rest."

For the next two weeks, Kangoma toured the entire city of Atlanta in a taxi with his four soldiers in the backseat. They went through every project and every neighborhood. He'd gotten them familiar with back streets and showed them how to get away on feet and use the Marta for an escape route if they had to. Today, they all went to A-Town records and studios, and met up with Hammer and Young Hollywood. They were in Hammer's favorite sitting area, and females were walking around serving champagne and Cuban cigars.

Young Hollywood was holding a solo conversation with the artists, Quick and Mossburg, near one of the pool tables.

Hammer greeted Kangoma with a hug and then Moyo with

a firm hand shake. "How you doing, Moyo?" Hammer asked him, still holding his hand.

Moyo stared up at Hammer. He bowed his head slightly. "I'm doing good."

Hammer repeated his process with Nzile next, then Biko and Kimani, greeting them all in the same fashion. They took seats in the leather chairs, with Hammer and Kangoma sitting next to each other.

He lit up a cigar and looked back at Quick and Mossburg. "Are y'all gonna join us?" he asked.

The two of them walked over and found a seat. Hammer looked around the room, making eye contact with everyone. The room fell silent and he casually pulled on his cigar, flipped his head back and exhaled the smoke. "Where are the twins?" he asked Young Hollywood.

His eyes beamed directly at him. "The fish market is being renovated. Apple Head had to stay back, and Muffin is working on that other move we talked about last night."

Hammer nodded, thought about their conversation, and then looked around at his close-knit crew. They were the strength. Hammer was indeed a thinker and a hard worker, and even more, he admired the power move that his son had made by bringing in the African soldiers. Silence hung in the air for the next few minutes as he allowed his mind to wander.

He looked at Young Hollywood. "I think the young ones here should stay on the ranch. That way, they will not be seen, and they'll have a secluded area to train." He looked at Kangoma and pulled on his cigar. "It's mandatory they receive an education."

Kangoma nodded. "I have that taken care of," he said.

The room fell silent again. Somebody's stomach growled loud enough for everyone to hear. "Damn, somebody hungry?"

Quick touched his stomach. "That be me," he said jokingly.

Again, Hammer nodded. "This shouldn't take long. My reason for calling this brief meeting is to let you all know that Wood, my son right here..." He pointed his cigar at Young Hollywood, and then he went on. "Will be taking over A-Town Records and Studio."

He looked at Kangoma and they communicated with their eyes. Kangoma knew this day was coming, and he definitely thought it to be a wise move. The men broke their stare, and Hammer's eyes went back to Young Hollywood. "You wanna say something?"

Young Hollywood stood up and moved around the room, shaking everyone's hand, one at a time. When he got to Hammer, he gave him a hug and whispered in his ear, "When I make my decision, you'll have the final say, regardless of what. How can our opponent checkmate us if they never see the king on the board?"

"The difference between the opponent and us is that we're the only ones that has a board full of kings. Everybody on our team should think like a king, and when you put that seed in their head, they'll move like a king. Then they'll bring in their own loyal rooks and pawns and knights." He paused and whispered in his ear even lower. "And most importantly, know the value of the queen."

"I was waiting on that," Young Hollywood said as he turned around and faced the circle. "The least we can do is throw a party for the city."

Hammer nodded, and then he said, "I agree."

21

A week later, an exclusive party was held in the Fox
Theatre. They'd rented out the entire theatre,
including the ballrooms. The party was filled with
over five hundred women from all walks of life. Some of them
wore long black weave and some wore their hair cut low,
sparkly dresses and stilettos. Athletes and celebrities, groupies,
pimps, gangstas and even some movie stars had come out this
evening on behalf of Hammer and the Governor, to show their
respect for Young Hollywood.

When the music stopped, a local comedian from Atlanta
named Shawty Pimp took to the stage in a Brooks Brothers suit,
and Salvatore Ferragamo shoes. When he grabbed the microphone, he scanned the audience of nearly two thousand
people. "Good evening ladies and gents, we're glad to have y'all
out here tonight on behalf of my young playa potna, Young
Hollywood."

The audience exploded into pandemonium, clapping and
cheering. He went on. "Now, some of you may not know Young
Hollywood, but I do. I met the nigga when he was three years
old. At the time, I was ten, and when I say this nigga was born a

gangsta. Man, when I say he's been a fool since he was three. Three goddamnit." He shouted, jumping up and down.

Laughter filled the room at the way Shawty Pimp talked. He had an irritating voice, but he was silly sounding. He took the microphone away from his mouth and placed his hands on his hip until the audience quieted down. He dropped his head and began shaking it side to side, desperately trying to hold his laugh.

When he looked up and faced the sea of people, he saw camera flashes here and there. Then he said, "So I'm ten years old, my older brother is twelve at the time, and we out here making mud pies. Everybody know 'bout mud pies. So after we hooked up our mud pies, we hear the ice cream man truck coming round the cona. Neither one of us got no money, mind you. So the ice cream truck cruised on past us. We sad and shit, then out of nowhere, we see a lil' nigga come around the cona on a Green Machine. He changing gears and shit, hauling ass behind the ice cream truck. Lil' nigga zoom straight past us, flagging down the ice cream truck. So the truck stop, and Young Hollywood step out of his Green Machine and run up on the ice cream man with a real gun. Me and my brother lookin' at each other. Then we hear a shot go off and the ice cream man come running from the truck and shoot straight past us."

He paused and motioned for something to drink. A slim female brought him a one liter plastic bottle of Evian water. After he removed the top and took a swallow, he scanned the crowd again, and even laughed at himself before he went on. "Remember, the lil' nigga is only three years old doin' this shit. So he comes down from the ice cream truck with his gun in one hand and a Push Up in the other. He get back in his Green Machine and ride past us real slow and say, "Yawl niggas ain't seen me either. I don't normally leave no witnesses."

The crowd went into laughter again, followed by explosive clapping. Then a 40-foot Matrix theatrical projection screen appeared behind him. "Ladies and gentlemen. Y'all give a round of applause for the A-Town Veteran, Young Hollywood."

When Shawty Pimp exited the stage, the lights went down and the 40-foot screen popped on, showing the front entrance of the Fox. Then a cocaine white Maybach pulled up with white interior. The camera went to the inside and showed Young Hollywood and Sasha in the backseat. They were both dressed in all white everything. He looked into the camera and raised a champagne glass. "There's nothing like achieving greatness," he said with a smile. "Are y'all having a good time tonight?"

The audience clapped and cheered again. Young Hollywood smiled. "I like that. Well, as y'all know, I'm the CEO of A-Town Records. Raising hell from Hollywood Court projects as a youngster, I've been through the trenches, and now I'm on the next, like my dude, Hov, would say."

The audience clapped again. The Maybach's rear door came open and the audience could see everything on the big screen. A huge bouncer opened the door on Sasha's side. She smiled and stepped out of the Maybach. The cameraman filmed her from head-to-toe; her body was curved perfectly.

When Young Hollywood stepped out, he was holding a $50,000.00 personalized bottle of Pernod Ricard Pierre Jouet Champagne in one hand, and the glass in the other. The red carpet was rolled out, and female groupies in tight fitting clothes cheered from behind the velvet ropes. Young Hollywood surveyed the entire front of the Fox Theatre as paparazzi flashed their cameras at him and Sasha.

"Mr. Terry Keys," the reporter said into his handheld microphone.

Young Hollywood paused and looked directly into the lens of the camera. He had a professional manner and clean appearance. Smiling, he leaned into the microphone. "No further questions." he said jokingly.

The reporter smiled. "I see you're in high spirits. How does it feel to come home from prison and be awarded the position of CEO of one of the most successful record labels in Atlanta?"

"Not better than being rewarded to be back with my family." He winked at the camera and walked off next to Sasha.

They entered the theatre and were escorted into the Egyptian Ballroom where the closest friends and family were. The space was decorated with elegance, including a huge champagne waterfall in the center of the room. Professional musicians were on standby, romantically candle lit tables were spread out, and the best of the best caterers had prepared more than enough exotic dishes.

Young Hollywood got a standing ovation that was led off by Hammer and the Governor. He and Sasha were led to a long corporate marble top table that sat at least forty people. In this room, everyone was casually dressed in expensive attire. Young Hollywood went around the table to each and every person and gave them a firm handshake or either a hug. He hugged Vincent and Vincent Jr, then Poe Boy and Diamond. There were three middle aged Muslims standing next to each other in tuxedos and Kofis. He didn't know them personally, but they were down with the team, and very well respected throughout Atlanta.

He smiled when he got to the twins, Apple Head and Muffin. He noticed Kangoma and the young soldiers were nowhere to be found. Then he got to the Governor and his wife; they were both approaching sixty, and the most respected in the room. Young Hollywood hugged them both and thanked them for coming out. Finally, he got to Hammer and Atiya. They looked stunning together. She wore a backless gown, with a huge diamond and platinum chain around her neck, and flawless diamond earrings that sparkled every time she moved.

Young Hollywood hugged her first and kissed her cheek

with a smile. "You look beautiful," he whispered in her ear. And he meant it with respect.

She gave him a grin and a kiss. When he departed from his stepmother, he went to Hammer and they stared each other in the eye, both of them smiling from ear-to-ear. They embraced, and the crowd clapped again while they enjoyed their emotional moment. This was like a dream come true for both of them. Their past was dangerous, and even more ruthless, with the knowledge they shared. This was their moment.

Cameras flashed throughout the huge room, recording the poignant scene between father and son. When they separated, Young Hollywood looked across the room at the many different faces. A huge black velvet curtain to his right separated and started to open, revealing another room full of people.

Shawty Pimp walked up and handed him the microphone.

Hammer leaned in his ear. "Take the stage, it's your show."

With the microphone in hand, he walked to the stage and moved up the side steps. He scanned the huge audience of people that were all staring at him and waiting for him to speak.

"First of all, I wanna thank all you beautiful people for coming out tonight," he said. The room filled with applause, along with a few whistles. Cameras flashed uncontrollably as Young Hollywood went on. "A lot of you probably don't know who I am, and maybe you may have heard a couple of Westside street tales about me." His eyes scanned the crowd; some faces were familiar and some weren't.

The audience was quiet and eagerly listening to what he had to say.

"I came up in Hollywood Court Projects with guidance from hustlas and gangstas. I inherited them traits at twelve years old. My father..." He looked over at Hammer and said into the microphone, "Can you come up here for a brief moment?"

Hammer stood up and the crowd erupted with thunderous applause as he made his way to the stage. Once on stage, Young Hollywood shook Hammer's hand and then looked out into the audience. "This man right here is the greatest man, father and person on the face of this earth."

The audience went wild again.

"This is my father, Rufus "Hammer" Hayes. He's now the Co-CEO of A-town Records and Studios, because he made me the CEO. This is the man that I strive to be like. I'll never try to outdo him, because he's the master. So y'all give a nice round of applause for my father, myself, my family, and yourself." He spit out his words carefully, and allowed a small smile to escape. His white veneers flashed and sparkled, at the adoring crowd.

Young Hollywood and Hammer then left the stage and snaked their way through the sea of people, shaking hands with NBA players, rappers, R&B singers, and a couple of politicians here and there. Beautiful women were looking sexy and seductive as they passed by.

Young Hollywood paused at a familiar face, the female that he'd seen in magazines and on BET so many times while he was in prison. Her slanted eyes and beautiful skin was flawless. He took her hand and politely kissed it softly while looking directly in her eyes. Before he could get a word out of his mouth, Hammer pulled up on him and threw his arm around his neck.

He extended his hand to her, disrupting Young Hollywood. "Good evening." Hammer told her, then added, "Enjoying yourself tonight?"

She smiled. "Yes, I am."

Without another word, Hammer guided Young Hollywood away from her and they moved on through the crowd. Thirty minutes later, they were back at their table as clean professional waiters walked around with leather back menus and placed them on the tables. Young Hollywood was sitting next to Sasha. She smiled at him and they shared a brief kiss.

"Better than ever," he whispered to her.

The head chef came over; she was a slim, petite German woman in her late forties. She wore a toque on her head and her ocean blue eyes complemented her smooth radiant skin. She went to Hammer and bowed her head. "Good evening, Mr. Hayes. I'm your executive chef, and as you can see from the menu, we'll be serving Muscovy duck breast with braised Napa cabbage, or optional roasted duck drizzled in mango sauce. We've prepared a six-course tasting dinner for your immediate friends and family. All of the food is fresh, nothing refrigerated, Mr. Hayes."

She clapped her hands above her head two quick times and a line of waiters in snow white uniforms, and kerchiefs around their necks appeared with several chrome utility carts. They first served exotic soups in espresso cups and brought out vintage imported wines. Everyone at the table received their own separated dish of lobster risotto and lop de mer. Hammer was impressed, and so was Young Hollywood, as expensive Cuban Havana cigars were served on glass trays along with razor snips.

Hammer was in a daze as he watched his son enjoy his meal. He saw him close his eyes and shake his head side-to-side, as if the food was out of this world delicious. Hammer tasted the food himself. The garlic, the butter, the olive oil and Parmesan flavors exploded inside his mouth.

"Damn, this shit is good," he said.

Atiya looked over at him. A smirk was on her face, as if she was telling him to watch his mouth. Hammer leaned over and kissed her cheek. She smiled and whispered in his ear, "I love you."

He whispered back in hers, "I love you too." And he meant every word of it.

The next course was Muscovy duck breast that had been imported straight from South America. The plates were neatly decorated with layers of meat, carrots and potatoes; small portions was how the entrees came out. Young Hollywood tasted a piece of the boneless Muscovy duck and the expression on his face reflected his opinion that the meat was some of the best he'd ever tasted in his life. With a mouth full, he looked up and waved his hand for one of the peon cooks.

One of the cooks noticed Young Hollywood's motion. He was a black guy who appeared to be in his early twenties, no moustache, and wire frame glasses. He wore chef pants and clogs, a fancy cotton chef jacket, and a toque sat perfectly on top of his head. When he finally got to Young Hollywood, he put on the calmest face and flashed a smile. "How may I help you this evening, sir?"

Young Hollywood stared at the man from his sitting position, then he stood up and extended his hand out to the cook. They exchanged a firm handshake. "What's good, pimp?" Young Hollywood asked him.

"I'm wonderful, sir. How are you doing?" The cook replied, holding very professional eye contact.

"This Muscovy duck breast shit is off da chain, brah."

"Thank you, sir. I'm glad that our services have satisfied you."

Young Hollywood patted his shoulder. "I may need you to do a private dinner for my family in the near future."

"I'm not in the position to take the offer, sir. However, I'll speak with the head chef or either the manager for your private banquet," the cook said.

Young Hollywood nodded and sat back down next to Sasha. His eyes swept around the room and he noticed how peaceful everything was, he was just enjoying life with family and friends.

The peon cook had disappeared, and within ten minutes,

he was back with a chrome platter and glass cover. He went straight to Young Hollywood with the warmest smile.

He removed the top and revealed a handmade dessert that was drizzled with rich, warm butterscotch. Young Hollywood tasted it without hesitation, and then he eased his fork into it and fed Sasha a bite also. They both nodded their heads approvingly. He looked back at the cook and asked him, "Who made this?"

The cook smiled. "I did, sir. And I also just got approved to do your personal dinner if you still want me to."

"Definitely." Young Hollywood exchanged numbers with the young cook, and in minutes, he was gone.

Young Hollywood had just met Sabertooth, Six Nine's main henchman.

22

Nearly eighteen months had passed since Sabertooth set off on his journey to become a chef, or at least obtain his Culinary Arts certificate. Six Nine thought it would look good on his resume, and Sabertooth took off. For the first month, he got a small dish washing gig at an all you can eat Chinese restaurant, just so he could get the feel of a kitchen and washing huge pots and pans. He mingled with the Chinese cooks, learned about egg rolls, and watched them prepare Sushi and flavorful chicken wings using more than three exotic recipes. His second month there, he was fired for making a pass at the wife of the owner.

A week later, he caught a job working pots and pans for a jazz club out in Decatur, working a three compartment sink and busting his ass with a Mexican dude and another black guy. After three days, he was gone. He applied for a job at the Applebee's on Cascade road, and caught his first cook position. In three months, he felt as if he knew the entire business of cooking.

He had quit and contacted Six-Nine over the phone from the V.I.P section at Strokers. Six Nine answered the phone and heard the loud noise in the background. "What's good, pimp?" he said over the loud music of Trick Daddy in the background.

"Shawty, man dis cook shit ain't workin'. I ain't feelin' it." Sabertooth said, as he caressed the round pretty ass of a female who was dancing in front of him. Her exotic perfume seeped up his nose.

"Where you at now?" Six Nine asked from the other end.

"At Strokers, jus relaxin' a moment."

"Well, take you a break, pimp. Get you a bitch or two, get a room at the Ritz, matter of fact, get an executive suite and I'll meet you there in about an hour."

"Sound 'bout right." Sabertooth ended his call and sipped Courvoisier XO from a glass. He stared out in a daze, allowing the music to soak into him. Finally, he grabbed the female's hand that was dancing before him. She turned and faced him; her soft pecan complexion glowed under the fluorescent lights. She never stopped moving to the beat. "Get a friend," he said. "We leavin."

No more than forty minutes later, Sabertooth was pulling into the parking lot of the Ritz in an Ocean blue Range Rover with two extravagant looking females. Relaxed and enjoying the soothing sound of Kem coming through the speakers, he weaved the Range, creeping at a steady pace. The female in the front seat looked toward him. "You don't talk much, do you?"

Sabertooth's eyes shifted toward her; his mouth pressed closed. Then, from the corner of his eye, he noticed a set of flashing headlights. He snapped his head in that direction and put his foot on the brake pedal. Staring at the unfamiliar car that was parked in a space in reverse, he knew it was Six Nine behind the wheel.

Sabertooth took the empty parking space next to him. He left the Range Rover running, got out, walked around to the passenger side of the Malibu, got in, and closed the door behind him.

Six Nine looked at him, staring down his hawk-like nose. "What's good, shawty?" Six Nine asked.

Sabertooth shook his head slightly, looking like he'd been defeated. "This cookin' shit, brah."

There was a short silence between the two of them, then Six Nine said, "We can't ruin a magnificent layout." He leaned closer. "This is where our bond seals to an unbreakable point. When we fuckin' wit a nigga like Hammer, it's like a chess game. Your moves have to be planned and seen before you even touch a piece on the board."

"That shit overrated, pimp. I can kill that nigga without going through all the extra bullshit."

"Yeah, I'm sure you can, but you'll be buried within twenty four hours, nigga, unless you wanna be labeled as a suicide bomber." He paused. "Other than that, it'll have to be done this way."

Sabertooth pinched the bridge of his nose. He went into deep thought, and began playing everything back in his head. *Move in silence*, he once heard Six Nine tell him. *Kill all your enemies and you don't have to worry about keeping them close.* Another famous Six Nine quote. Sometimes you have to appear to lose in order to win. The world is filled with pawns, rooks, and bishops. If you ever want to meet a king, know yourself.

He finally looked over at Six Nine as his adrenaline pumped through his veins. He held his hand up and Six Nine gripped it.

"I gotcha, pimp."

"Good business." Six Nine shot back, and then he asked, "What about ya company?"

Sabertooth shook his head. "I'm good, you can deal with 'em. I'ma get me a room and get some rest."

The following morning, Sabertooth awoke alone in a huge

antique bed, surrounded by eggshell marble at the Ritz Carlton. He wiped the sleep from his eyes and glanced at his watch. It read 8:37 A.M. Still feeling drained, Sabertooth closed his eyes and allowed his head to fall back to the soft pillow.

He slept for another hour and was up again, his eyes sharp. Rising from the colossal mahogany four-poster bed, he stood, stretched, and let out a light yawn. After Sabertooth showered, he dressed in the same gear from the night before and brushed his teeth.

Downstairs in the lobby, the atmosphere was live and energetic. Hotel guests were coming and going. He got to the entrance doors and an older white female brushed past him at an alarming pace. She was a slim petite German woman who wore an Egyptian cotton chef's coat. Just as she made it through the glass doors, she snatched off her toque. Sabertooth immediately recognized her as a chef and picked up his pace. He quickly caught up with her.

"Excuse me, Miss." He said in a polite tone.

The lady stopped and turned around. She trained her eyes on Sabertooth, nearly frowning as she looked him up and down. Her hair was auburn and pinned up in a neat bun, her lips were thin and rose red, and her eyes were a light honey color.

"How may I help you?" she asked.

"Question one, do you work here?"

"Answer one, I just quit," she snapped and then she turned. "Sorry, but I have a full schedule." She began walking off.

Sabertooth got in stride with her and said, "I'm interested in being a chef, but I need professional training from someone like you." He moved in front of her and stopped her in her tracks.

She put her hands on her hips and rolled her eyes. "Listen, sir. I'm not interested."

"I got sixty thousand cash if you teach me how to cook on a professional level like you."

"I'm a three-star Michelin ranking," she said. "You'll have to be very disciplined and highly trained for ranking like that."

"I'll throw in another offer. Teach me, then I'll front the funds for you to start your own business. Whatever the price may be."

A smile spread across her face. "I'm sure you're kidding, right?" she asked him.

"Just give me two hours of your time. We can go back inside the hotel while I make a call, and I'll get your money within an hour."

She became more relaxed. "So are we gonna introduce ourselves?"

Sabertooth took her hand and kissed the back of her fingers. "I'm your student."

She blushed again, and in a soft voice, she said, "I'm your teacher."

23

Hammer and Young Hollywood rode alone in the rear of a stretch limousine, both casually dressed on a beautiful Sunday afternoon, surrounded by soft black leather and glossy oak wood. Kangoma was in the front driving. The traffic began to slow down, and Hammer pressed a button on the panel and spoke to Kangoma through a mini intercom.

"No traffic jams, if you can avoid it." Hammer said.

Kangoma's voice came back through the panel. "Everything is about to stop, looks like a bad accident up ahead."

Hammer looked at Young Hollywood, and Young Hollywood returned his stare, both lost in thought. Young Hollowyood thought back to the first time that they'd met.

"You the Hammer from Atlanta?" were his first words that he'd asked him from his cell.

"Who da fuck is you? Askin' bout Hammer."

"You hear me?" Hammer said again, bringing Young Hollywood back to the present.

Young Hollywood smiled, his attention was back on

Hammer. "My bad, I was just trippin' on how gangsta you sounded when we first met down in Reidsville."

Hammer smiled. "What you mean sounding?" He allowed a slight laugh to exit his mouth. He folded his arms across his chest, then he said. "I remember you comin' in, talking 'bout. Yeah, I'm Young Hollywood, zone one, Hollywood Court."

"Now that shit was gangsta."

"You was scared to death, go ahead and tell the truth. I swear I won't tell nobody."

"Scared?" Young Hollywood's facial muscles tensed. "A'int neva scared like Bone Crusha."

Hammer removed a cigar from a glossy wooden box built inside the console and slid it underneath his nose to smell the fresh tobacco aroma. Then he handed it to Young Hollywood and removed another one for himself, his sharp eyes fixed on his son.

"This keep it real Sunday." Hammer said while flicking his lighter and cupping his hand around the flames and lighting his cigar.

With a small smirk on his face, Young Hollywood finally said, "I was nervous at first, but I wasn't scared like most niggas be." Then he reached for the lighter and lit his own cigar. He pulled on it until it came to life. "What about you?"

"What, scared?"

Young Hollywood smiled. "Damn right." He said, and then added, "It's keep it real, Sunday."

"I wouldn't give a damn if it was keep it real Monday, Tuesday, and Wednesday. Yeah, I had butterflies just a little bit. That happens anytime you step into a new atmosphere. And you right, you don't necessarily have to be scared. That's just like if they called me right now and told me to come on the Oprah Winfrey show. I'ma be nervous than a motha'fucka."

They laughed together, smoked their cigars and exchanged

more game and business plans. No more than thirty minutes later, they pulled up to an estate. At the entrance, Nicole Terry was waiting by the iron gates at the mouth of the long winding driveway in a gray halter top, gray nylon shorts and New Balance running shoes. She was jogging in place when the limousine came to a halt. Nicole punched in a security code on the keypad and the steel entrance barrier began to roll open on its track.

Kangoma eased the limousine inside far enough so the gate would close. When the gate finally closed, Hammer rolled down his window where Nicole was standing. She was pouring sweat and her nipples were hard, pressing against the wet fabric of her halter-top.

"Hello there," she chirped happily, staring directly into Hammer eyes with a smile.

The cigar smoke exited the limousine and streamed into her face. She fanned briefly, then her eyes went to Young Hollywood. She smiled again, her teeth even and white. "So we finally get a chance to meet," she said to him, then she added, "My, my, you sure look like your father."

Without a word, Hammer checked his watch. He wasn't pressed for time, but he definitely wanted to go handle his business. "Get in, Ms. Terry."

She ran around to the other side of the limousine and got into the front seat with Kangoma. Out of respect, she wasn't about to ride in the rear with Hammer and Young Hollywood, pouring sweat. Five minutes later, Kangoma pulled the limousine up to the front of the guesthouse. Kangoma killed the engine and stepped out.

Young Hollywood and Hammer stepped out also, and all three of them fell in stride. Inside the four-bedroom guesthouse, the four African soldiers were sitting in the living room playing Madden with the PlayStation 3 on a huge seventy-inch flat screen. Leather chairs and sofas were spread around in multiple configurations. The kids were kicked back and relaxed.

The four of them stood up when Hammer, Young Hollywood and Kangoma entered.

Hammer fanned his hand dismissively, moved over toward one of the leather double stuffed loveseats, and sat down.

Young Hollywood found himself a seat next to Kimani, and Kangoma went into the kitchen.

Hammer looked at Nzile and motioned for him to come sit next to him. On the surface, he was a heartless killer, but in Hammer's eyes, he was just a child who needed guidance. When he sat down next to Hammer, Hammer put his arm around his neck and pulled him to him, showing respect and affection.

Biko, Kimani and Moyo looked at that and instantly became surprisingly happy.

"How you doin'?" Hammer asked Nzile.

Nzile looked up at him, his eyes were bright and wide, and his oval shaped face was expressionless. Hammer recognized his pain, and knew the history of their culture. Nzile only nodded his head without saying a word, as if he couldn't talk unless he was commanded to.

When he didn't respond, Hammer politely stood up and excused himself. He walked into the kitchen looking for Kangoma, but he wasn't there. Moving toward the glass patio doors, he saw Kangoma outside on the patio overlooking the wide spacious manicured yard. Hammer opened the glass door, walked outside, and stood next to him.

Kangoma looked at him for a split second then trained his eyes back to the green manicured lawn. Something was on his mind. He looked at Hammer again, and Hammer exchanged the same look. "I was just inside talking with Nzile. Well, let me rephrase that. I was talking, and for some reason, he refused to respond."

"He's only a soldier, Hammer. A trained killer and nothing more. Nzile is trained only to respond to my command."

In an even tone, Hammer said, "I think we should remove Nzile from the list. He's young, and needs to be preparing for a bigger position."

"You got to understand our culture, Hammer." Kangoma shot back. "He was born to die in the battle field."

"I understand everything you're saying. I understand your culture, and I definitely know we're responsible for our circle only. So, as of now, you'll no longer train Nzile for war. The others, we'll keep in position."

Kangoma squinted; he took a deep breath while looking at Hammer.

"As you wish." Out of respect and loyalty, Kangoma would never go against Hammer. Or would he?

24

O ut in Buckhead, nestled deep in the woods, was a $900,000 dollar Georgian style estate filled with Corvettes, Porsches and a couple of Range Rovers. Inside one of the three vacuumed sealed garages were three Lamborghinis owned by Six Nine. The first one was a deep midnight blue, with custom powder blue interior.

He drove that only when he visited Macon, Georgia, and kicked it with Crip gangs on the Westside. The next one was high glossed, candy apple red with black interior. Of course, this was his favorite one, because many of his associates were members of the blood gangs that were slowly but surely turning Atlanta into their hub.

Last, but not least, was his flashy black lambo. This one was for when he mingled with the Gangster Disciples out of Chicago and there in Atlanta.

The man wasn't stupid by far, this was called having good game and street social skills.

Tonight, the inside of the home was crawling with members of his own crew: Black Cartel men as well as women. One room in particular, half the size of a high school gym, was polished with overstuffed leather furniture at one end of the room, surrounding a two hundred pound, glossy black marble table made in the shape of a huge A, the exact logo from the Braves cap. The walls were covered with dark cherry wood paneling. Running a long parallel angle, and at the other end, Six Nine sat in an in-ground Jacuzzi, sipping promethazine cough syrup with half naked models-exotic dancers, some with painted on bikinis. They served drinks on silver platters and passed out cigars, while some rolled up exotic marijuana. Two females were standing in the far corner tongue kissing and giggling amongst themselves.

On the other side of the Jacuzzi with two females was Sabertooth, looking straight into Six Nine's untrusting eyes. They were just relaxing, but business was never far from their minds. They began talking in codes about Hammer and Young Hollywood.

Six Nine said to Sabertooth, "You know, I'm a strong believer in killing the head and the body will fall."

Sabertooth had his arms outstretched around the edge of the Jacuzzi. The females were playfully splashing water across his face and on each other. He gave them both a 'stop playing' stare. "So what about the Jr.?" He asked Six Nine, referring to Young Hollywood.

Six Nine twisted his face, unsure of the decision he was ready to make. "See, pimp ain't no thinker." He thought and allowed the words to register. "I know I can finesse him and rock his ass to sleep. Long as you put the full court press on the German chick to set up the luncheon, and then yo' special recipe." He looked down his Hawk nose.

With a serious look, and eyes turning into slits, Sabertooth nodded. "Niggas won't never see this one coming."

"And that's basically with anything in life." He sipped on his Hawaiian Punch and Promethazine-codeine cough syrup, then he went on. "Just like tomorrow, if I go meet this nigga and I get offed in the process." He paused and pondered what he was about to say, and decided it wouldn't sound right. "Never mind."

"What was you about to say?" Sabertooth asked.

Six Nine replied. "Something stupid." His eyes were getting heavy and he decided to get out of the water. Standing in a pair of black silk boxers, he looked around the room and stepped out. A half-naked Asian girl had a terry cloth robe waiting for him. After he put it on, he kissed her forehead, walked to the other end of the room, and took a seat in one of the over-stuffed leather chairs.

His vision was becoming blurry, so he took one last sip of his Hawaiian Punch and Promethazine and quickly set it down in a marble cup holder and kicked back in a relaxed-comfortable position. His eyes batted closed, but he tried desperately to fight the sleep. Now the voices around him sounded far away, as if the other people were screaming from a tunnel or a well. Perhaps voices slowing down and then moving faster. Then he succumbed to a deep sleep.

BOOK 3

YOUNG HOLLYWOOD/SIX NINE

18 Months later
IT TAKES GREAT TALENT AND SKILLS TO CONCEAL
ONE'S TALENT AND SKILLS
LA ROCHEFOUCALD, 1613-1680

25

"Power requires self-discipline," Young Hollywood said to Sasha as she pulled into the parking lot of an exclusive wine bar & bistro called the Grape at Atlantic Station. Behind the steering wheel of a clean S class Mercedes Benz, she eased in front of a waiting valet and turned her smile towards Young Hollywood.

"And I definitely agree with you," she said as she stopped the car completely and eased the shift into park. "In the book, Forty-Eight Laws of Power, Robert Green seems to stress Law thirty five to me a lot."

"So you saying I'm not a patient man?"

"I'm saying I want you to think like Michael Corleone and not Sonny Corleone." She delivered her words carefully.

Young Hollywood smiled at the statement, knowing she'd remembered that from the movie *The Godfather*, that they'd watched so many times when they were younger. Then he said, "See, Michael could think." He touched his chest. "And I definitely can think."

She opened her door. The interior lights highlighted her beautiful features. The honey toned lipstick seemed to caress her lips, and her olive green eyes stared at him with confidence. With her pretty hair hanging past her shoulders, she leaned over toward Young Hollywood and kissed his cheek. The Jasmine scent she wore opened his nostrils. She pulled away from him and stepped out in hip clinging slacks, an earth toned silk button up blouse, and low heeled Jimmy Choo's.

Young Hollywood's arrogance made him wear something simple, denim jeans, brown leather Polo boots, and a simple $700 Polo shirt. He eased on a pair of rimless, platinum Cartier frames with lavender tint octagon shaped lenses. He completed the look with one platinum pinky ring and a leather band watch.

When he stepped out into the cool night air, his shirt rattled from the wind. He stood there for a moment and just looked around at the well-lit and beautifully designed structure of the Atlantic Station.

The valet moved the car. Young Hollywood pulled up next to Sasha and they fell in stride together as they headed into the Grape's sophisticated and contemporary atmosphere. They were escorted into a private dining room where they'd pre-arranged a customized wine tasting for four.

Five minutes after they were seated, Six Nine entered with an NBA ball player swagger, with a five-carat yellow diamond sitting heavy on each earlobe, and dressed in linen slacks, dress shoes, and a wrinkled cream linen shirt. Next to him was a female who stood six feet tall and six-three in her heels. Her skin was black and smooth, like expensive dark chocolate. Her hair was cut short like a little boy, with a sharp tapeline, very clean and professional looking. Her eyes were slanted, and when she smiled, her teeth were evenly white and pretty.

The dark female stared directly at Sasha. Sasha stood with a smile and extended her hand. The girl shook it. They exchanged smiles and then a hug. "My name is Sasha."

The dark skinned girl looked Sasha in her eyes while holding her hand.

"My name is Amber," she said in a high-pitched southern tone as they sat down together.

Young Hollywood stood up, he and Six Nine locked hands, then a quick embrace. "What's good, Pimp?" Young Hollywood asked.

"Same ole shit." Six Nine shot back, and then he introduced Young Hollywood to Amber. "This is my fiancé, Amber."

Young Hollywood extended his hand out to her. They stared into each other's eyes for a brief second, as if they knew each other and were quickly trying to conceal it.

"I'm Young Hollywood," he said, then he released her long fingers, sliding his thumb against her pinky.

She smiled even more. "A-Town records, right?"

"Correct." He said, and then he turned and introduced Sasha to Six-Nine.

"This is my wife, Sasha."

Six Nine shook her hand and kissed the back of it. She blushed, then he said, "As you know, I'm Six Nine."

"Nice to meet you. I've heard so much about you, it's like I've been knowing you for years."

Six Nine laughed aloud. "I'll keep that in mind."

The four of them sat around a large round table underneath the Edison lights, which gave off a warm glow. A clean cut waiter approached their table with a stainless steel tray carrying four crystal wine glasses. Two other waiters brought a separate bottle of wine. The first bottle was Volpi Moscato, and the second one was called Fat Monk Pinot Noir. As the waiters poured their glasses, Six Nine looked over at Young Hollywood. "So, how ya old man doin'?" He asked him and grabbed his champagne glass.

Young Hollywood, Sasha and Amber grabbed their champagne glasses also. Young Hollywood held his glass up, inviting a toast. Six Nine clinked his glass against his, and then all four glasses touched one another. Young Hollywood said in a low calm voice. "Hammer is doin much better." His eyes locked in on Six Nine, honest and sincere.

Six Nine caught his stare, but he quickly looked away from him. His eyes darted around the table, and when they got back to Young Hollywood, he said, "Damn, I'm glad to hear that. I heard ya'll caught up with the enemies."

Young Hollywood sipped on his wine, the taste was smooth and easy. Then he nodded and began telling Six-Nine what happened to Hammer.

26

I t happened over a year ago.

Young Hollywood had arranged a special dinner date for Hammer and Atiya at their estate.

Sabertooth, being the chef of the night, had brought out some of the best food that money could buy. Nzile, the youngest African soldier was sitting at the table as well, casually dressed and well mannered.

Hammer had taken a liking to him, and wanted to see him grow up and became something besides a trained killer. He'd enrolled him into a private school, and he was quickly becoming accustomed to the American culture. His choice of sport was soccer, and Hammer and the rest of the family had attended all of his games.

Inside the dimly lit dining room, the three of them sat around the formal table.

Atiya looked stunning, dressed in a strapless Donna Karan gown, with a multi-million dollar diamond and platinum necklace nestled against her soft skin. She looked up at Hammer. "Rufus," she said in a soft voice.

Hammer was going over some income statements from the record label, but he shifted his gaze from the paper and looked up at her. His facial muscles were as relaxed as possible, and his look answered her. All she did was blow him a kiss across the table. He smiled, then pretended to catch it and blew her the same kiss back. When she pretended to catch it, Nzile laughed at both of them and just shook his head.

When Sabertooth appeared in the dining room, he was dressed in chef pants, clogs, and a toque that made him look more professional than he was. With a kerchief around his neck, and the most innocent looking smile on his face, he greeted the three of them with a perfect smile and then a handshake.

When he shook Nzile's hand, he stared him directly in his eyes. Nzile sensed something alarming. A danger signal went off in his head as he held onto Sabertooth's hand.

Sabertooth didn't recognize his stare because he was just young and innocent. From the chrome utility cart, he removed the top and exposed three espresso cups filled with steaming hot exotic soups. He placed one in front of Atiya first. The aroma hit the air, playing with her nostrils. She smiled as she smelled the soup and then closed her eyes. Hammer got his next, and with the same results, the aroma hit his nose and his stomach growled.

"What's in it?" Hammer asked.

Sabertooth smiled and displayed his even white teeth. "Lobster, potatoes and carrots." he said in a professional tone. Then he gave Nzile his cup, carefully placing it directly in front of him.

Nzile's eyes went to the soup, then back to Sabertooth. His stare became more intense as he watched Sabertooth. Nzile picked up his spoon and extended the filled spoon out to Sabertooth.

Sabertooth, stared awkwardly at Hammer. His heart thumped harder inside his chest. Hammer didn't say one word. Sabertooth turned his attention back to Nzile. Nzile's stare turned deadly.

With a small smile, Sabertooth took the spoon from him and blew it carefully to cool it down, then he cleaned the spoon, making the soup disappear into his mouth.

When he swallowed, Nzile watched him carefully.

Nothing happened.

Sabertooth kissed the tip of his fingers and raised them into the air. "Magnificent." he said.

Hammer was satisfied.

Atiya was lost; she thought it was a magic trick. After they ate their soup, Sabertooth brought out French bread and thinly sliced Muscovy duck breast that was drizzled with sweet Mango sauce. It was neatly decorated and smelled overwhelmingly delicious. Nzile was the first one to bite into the Muscovy duck breast covered with the poison Mango sauce. The taste was unique, but nothing to convince him that the food was poison. Atiya bit into a piece of the meat next, and then Hammer broke off a piece of the French bread.

Sabertooth was nervous now. He went back toward the kitchen, disappearing from their sight.

When Hammer picked up a thin slice of the meat, Nzile felt a light warm feeling in his throat that was quickly turning into an uncomfortable heat. Just then, Atiya jerked her head forward, an acid vomit taste rising in her throat. Her body heated up instantly, and her eyes turned watery and red.

Nzile stood up and raced toward the kitchen in search of Sabertooth. The poison was in the bottom of his stomach now, and it quickly brought him to his knees.

Sabertooth saw him coming and produced a sharp knife. Angrily, he stepped toward Nzile, and Nzile forcefully kicked him in his groin. Sabertooth stumbled backwards, the pain was excruciating.

Nzile got back to his feet, realizing he was nearing death, something he didn't fear at all. He raced toward Sabertooth and Sabertooth plunged the knife into Nzile's stomach. Nzile held onto Sabertooth, grabbed him around his neck and pulled Sabertooth's face into his. He bit down on Sabertooth's bottom lip and grinded down until it was off, as a stream of blood sprayed. Then Nzile locked in on his nose, the cartilage crushing underneath his bite.

Sabertooth yelped like a wounded animal. His clean cooking uniform was now covered in dark blood. Nzile finally released him and fell to the floor like a sack of potatoes, with the knife wedged underneath his ribcage. Sabertooth stared over at him, his eyes wide with a mixture of fear and anger. From a duffel bag, he removed a small caliber semi-automatic and headed back towards the dining room.

Inside the dining room, Hammer was holding Atiya's head, placing his mouth on hers and performing mouth-to-mouth resuscitation. His eyes were showing his terror and panic as he watched his wife fight for her life. She was spitting up blood, her chest rising and falling. Fear poured from her eyes as she shook violently one hard time as the cyanide finally overpowered her.

Now, Hammer was feeling his own throat begin to swell, and it was hard for him to swallow.

He got to his feet, spun around and began moving his legs, running toward the bathroom. Just as he turned the corner, he bumped into Sabertooth and knocked him over. Sabertooth took three steps backwards and fired the gun just as he was falling. Hammer caught the bullet in his left shoulder. His adrenaline kept him moving forward and rushing straight toward Sabertooth.

Another shot went off. Hammer felt the searing pain pierce his thigh; he stumbled, and was knocked from his feet. Hammer looked at Sabertooth. His face was covered in blood, nearly unrecognizable. He grabbed Sabertooth by his pants legs and snatched him down.

Sabertooth lifted his leg and leveled the heel of his foot on Hammer's jaw. Struggling, he stood back up on his feet and aimed the gun at Hammer's head.

Nzile seemed to appear out of thin air and jumped on his back. He had a psychotic stare in his eyes and the same knife in his hand. With a loud roar, using the last amount of strength he had, he drove the knife through Sabertooth's neck and quickly removed it. He then plunged it through his eye socket.

Sabertooth's body went limp and fell to the floor, with Nzile still holding him around his neck. Moments later, they were both dead.

27

J ust listening to Young Hollywood tell the story had brought Sasha and Amber to tears. Young Hollywood stared at Six-Nine through his lavender tinted Cartiers. Six Nine sipped from his wine glass and toyed around with a cigar that he couldn't wait to light up. He looked at his missing finger and thought about Hammer. Smiling like hell on the inside, his saddened eyes went back to Young Hollywood, and he just shook his head in disbelief.

"Out of the blue?" he asked. "Was it a hit?"

"Definitely, it came for the inside. Our head henchman, Kangoma, was responsible. He hired the catering services that lame worked for."

"It's always a nigga that's close to you. The one you'll trust with your life." Six Nine responded.

Young Hollywood held up his glass and Six Nine tapped his glass against his.

Amber snuggled up against Six Nine, giving him her comforting woman's touch. He smiled at her and kissed her lips. Then he raised her hand where she wore a huge seven-carat diamond ring sitting on a mound of platinum.

He kissed her finger and ring, causing her to blush.

Sasha smiled. "You two look so good together." she said, then she asked, "I'm anxious to know how you two met."

"Pimpin' Six Nine." Young Hollywood said with a smile. He looked at Amber. "To contain a man with high standards such as his, you got to be unique."

Amber smiled. She was anxious to share her story with Young Hollywood and Sasha. She looked up at Six Nine, and with her eyes, she asked him if it was okay. He shrugged and smiled. Still smiling, he fired up his cigar and puffed on it until it came to life. "If you wanna let'em know how I swept you off your feet."

Amber rolled her eyes and sucked her teeth. "Anyway." She looped her arm through Six Nine's. Her eyes bright and beautiful. She looked over at Sasha; Sasha blushed at Amber in a friendly way. Everyone was actually glad that the street wars and beef were finally over. Amber sat up and cleared her throat. Her eyes darted from Sasha to Young Hollywood and then to Six Nine. He was cocked to the side and casually smoking his cigar.

Amber looked at Six Nine once more and began her story. "I moved to Georgia six months before Hurricane Katrina hit New Orleans..."

On this particular night, it was the grand opening of Six Nine's spot called Atlanta-Vegas. Six Nine had envisioned this idea one night while he was high on exotic marijuana and rolling on x-pills. But he never allowed his vision to become blurred when it came to him getting some money. Atlanta-Vegas, designed for millionaires and players. Exotic drinks they served, exotic women got in free on Thursdays and Saturdays. Membership required ownership of an exotic sports car. The sprawling establishment was designed to be an experience from the moment you pulled up in the parking lot. It wasn't just a regular parking lot. The valet took your car through an auto-

matic clear windowed wash for a spray down with low-pressure water.

The VIP room, a smaller version of the Sundial was panoramic glass enclosed, and rotated slowly, offering members a view of their exotic cars being soaped up and washed down by naked women. This view was from a tastefully appointed room, equipped with overstuffed large leather sofas and chairs, marble floors beneath a marble top table in the design of the letter A. As the room evolved, the huge bars came into view. One on each side, and stretching nearly the length of a football field. Then the cars would enter the inside of Atlanta-Vegas. The valet parked the clean sports car on the black carpet.

Six-Nine had invested close to seven million dollars in this establishment. He mainly catered to celebrities like T.I, Jeezy, Scarface, Baby and Slim, Yo Gotti, as well as the street millionaires and goons like himself.

The women poured in by the dozens in top of the line clothing from the best fashion houses. Six-Nine's office overlooked the entire club from the second floor like a skybox. Four huge bulletproof tinted windows lined the front. From where he stood, he could see the entire interior layout of the club. Being a connoisseur of fine intelligent looking women, he noticed a small commotion directly across from him in the upper deck VIP room.

Six Nine exited his office. His swagger was casual tonight. Dressed in a soft pink silk shirt, expensive dark denim jeans and soft pink alligator skin shoes. Despite being a certified killer, Six Nine was representing for his partner's auntie who was just diagnosed with breast cancer, and in honor of his mother who died of cancer when he was ten years old. Even with the cancer awareness symbol around his neck made of pink diamonds, he still found a way to be an arrogant son of a bitch.

Moving through the crowd and watching it open up for him made him feel like God. He quickly made his way to the small crowd of four females, two NBA players and three huge mean looking secu-

rity guards. One female who really caught Six Nine's attention was the slim, long legged black one, wearing her same boyish haircut and holding a champagne glass.

She smiled at Six Nine. "It was only an accident," she said. "I stumbled, some champagne wasted on his mink." She shrugged as if to say, 'minor.'

Six Nine looked at the ball player and extended his hand, not recognizing his face or what team he played for. "My apologies," he said a calm voice. "If you need me to reimburse you..."

"No, no... Everything Gucci." He responded, sounding like he couldn't believe that he was being insulted in a calm manner.

He touched Six Nine on his shoulder and stared him in his eyes. "Thanks for the offer," he said, and looked around at the three females. Something turned in his stomach about them, as if they were looking for trouble. He still managed a smile before he walked off with the other ball player behind him.

Six Nine's eyes went back to the females, each of them wearing colorful contact lenses. Six Nine extended his hand to the dark skinned one.

She grabbed his hand, noticed that his finger was missing, but didn't speak about it. "They call me Six Nine, I'm the owner."

"Well, they call me Amber, and I got to pee." She squeezed her legs together and anxiously moved side to side.

"Follow me," he told her, not even acknowledging the other two females.

Amber looked back at her three associates, and with a smile, she said, "See yawl bitches later." Then winked her eye.

Inside his office, he showed Amber to the bathroom while he went to the bar. Standing beside the shiny oak wood bar, he removed a blue dolphin x-pill and a high powered pain pill from a sandwich bag. He popped them both in his mouth and washed them down with a cold one-liter bottle of Evian spring water.

When Amber came from the bathroom, she was still holding a half-filled champagne glass. Looking around, she said, "This is nice, you would never see nothing like this in Mississippi."

Six Nine looked at her. "That's where you from?" He asked and began lighting a cigarette.

"Yes." She said, then she frowned and fanned her hand across her face. "Please, I can't stand smoke."

Six Nine twisted his face, looking at her in disbelief. He slowly snubbed the Newport out in a glass ashtray. "I don't normally do this," he said.

Amber's eyes saddened playfully, but a smile was on her lips. She walked behind the bar where Six Nine was standing. She sat her glass down on the counter top, looked up at Six Nine, stood on her toes and kissed him on his cheek. "Smoking is bad for your health anyway." Back down on her high heels, she picked up her champagne glass and sipped. Her seductive eyes stared up into his. "So, what's next?"

Six Nine, liking the conversation and definitely admiring her physical appearance, moved down to the other end of the bar and poured himself a glass of champagne. He looked back at her. "Why you wearing contact lenses?"

Another enticing smile. "And why can't my eyes be real?"

She moved closer to him, inches away from his face, her body pressed against his. She raised up on her tiptoes again.

Six Nine didn't move. His hands found the small of her waist and hers draped across his shoulders. When their lips touched, Six Nine tasted cotton candy. His hands slipped down and cuffed her soft round ass.

She pulled away from him. "I didn't tell you to touch my ass."

"Next, you gonna say you don't fuck on the first night."

"I don't," she said calmly.

"Out of respect, I wont push the issue then."

Through the walls, a song by Maxwell began to ease the mood. Six Nine was relaxing more, the pills were kicking in. He kissed Amber again, this time with a tongue. She nearly lost her breath, and relaxed in his powerful arms, easing her hands underneath his soft pink shirt, gently squeezing his muscles.

She felt a lump underneath his skin at the top of his back. "That's a bullet?" she whispered.

Without a word from Six Nine, he carefully eased his hand down the back of her pants, touching her lace thong. His long fingers were nearly at her vagina.

She removed his hand. "Answer my question."

Six Nine decided to take another route. He kissed her neck. "Yeah, I got shot," he finally said. He was rolling now, and beginning to feel himself just a little bit more.

Without warning, Amber cuffed Six Nine's ass. This time she kissed him violently. "Who shot you?" she asked between kisses.

"Who you work fa, First Forty-Eight?" He asked in a joking manner.

She laughed, really letting him know that she would never be a police, or anything near it. Then she finally said, "I'm a student, that's all."

"What school?"

"Georgia Perimeter College"

"Sho'nuff." Six Nine pulled her closer, and then, they began dancing to the Maxwell song. He whispered in her ear, "If I offend you, I'm sorry. But you must know that I have to search you to see if you're wired."

She stopped dancing, stepped away from him and gave him an angry stare.

"You bullshittin' right?" she asked.

Six Nine shook his head and his eyes were serious.

28

The arrival of their waiter temporarily halted the story. Six Nine looked at him and everyone was quiet, anticipating the rest of the story that he and Amber shared. Another waiter came out behind the first one. They brought a silver decorated tray of mini stuffed mushrooms, with another tray of Kettle Chips.

This time, their choice of wine was California Strawberry and Louis M. Martini Cabernet. Young Hollywood dug straight into the stuffed mushrooms, popping them in his mouth one at a time. "These mothafuckas taste good," he said to everyone.

Fresh champagne glasses etched with the Grape logo were set on the table.

Amber addressed the waiter. "For the four of us, would you please bring Vanilla Crème brûlée cheesecake?"

"No sweets for me," Sasha said to the waiter.

Amber looked at Sasha. "You gotta taste this, honestly." She smiled and grabbed Sasha's hand. "Sometimes it's hard to trust people you've just met, but please believe me on this."

Sasha was convinced. She looked toward the waiter and nodded with a smile.

The waiters left.

Six Nine reached over and grabbed a couple of stuffed mushrooms.

Young Hollywood looked at Amber and Six Nine, and then he said, "What happened next?"

Six-Nine popped his collar and gave Young Hollywood a look as if he couldn't believe he had asked him that question. "Straight to the Renaissance, the pool suite."

Amber, looking shy and innocent, sipped the California Strawberry from her glass, listening to Six Nine boast and brag. She sat her glass down and turned her attention on Six Nine, feeding him the mini mushrooms.

"Well, tell them the rest of the story after we got to the Renaissance."

Six Nine allowed a small innocent smile to play across his face. He looked at Young Hollywood then his eyes shifted to Sasha. They were both eagerly waiting, anticipating his next words. He looked at Amber; her eyes were seductive and sharp. "We didn't fuck."

Young Hollywood nearly yelled, "Ahhh man, pimp."

Sasha smiled and raised her champagne glass up to Amber. Amber returned the smile and raised her glass as well. They clinked their glasses in a toast.

Out the blue, Six Nine pointed his index finger. "But we did the next night."

Young Hollywood laughed and spit wine from his mouth, spraying the food and the table. Six Nine reared back, trying to avoid being hit, and he spilled champagne on his own clothes. "Damn." He stood up and caught himself before catching an attitude. He looked around the table. "Excuse me," he said, and went toward the bathroom.

Young Hollywood leaned over and kissed Sasha on her cheek. "Give me a minute, I'ma catch this bathroom," he whispered, trying to catch up with Six Nine.

She nodded and touched his chin. The whiskers in his goatee rubbed across her fingers. Then she kissed his lips and softly sucked his tongue. "I love you," she whispered.

Young Hollywood kissed her fingers and departed, moving through a maze of people, as Sasha watched him disappear.

"That's my angel," Sasha said in a low tone. "And I love him to death."

"I can tell," Amber said, looking directly at Sasha. She grabbed her wine glass and took a swallow. Then she said, "I wish I could say the same."

Shocked at her statement, Sasha looked at her in disbelief.

Inside the bathroom, Six Nine removed his linen shirt while standing in front of the wall-to-wall mirror. Now in a wife beater, he looked at his face, staring into his own eyes. Sometimes asking himself how did he make it this far. Then answering his own question. He mumbled to himself. "It takes great talent and skills to conceal one's talent and skills."

Young Hollywood pulled up next to him, punched the button on the hand sanitizer, and as he eased his hands underneath the chrome faucet, the water came on instantly. He looked over at Six Nine. "Talkin to ya self?"

Six Nine was wiping the wine spot on his shirt, but it was useless. He looked down at Young Hollywood. "You know what I was jus' thinkin' about?"

Young Hollywood began drying his hands with the paper towels. "Bout what, pimp?"

"Out of all the shit we went through in the last year, you know, fighting for our city against them New Orleans niggas... We still didn't never find out who Ambassador Black was."

"Man, niggas in the streets came up with that shit. Who ever seen this Ambassador Black? New Orleans niggas came with that bullshit."

Six Nine nodded, dug in his front pocket and removed two Oxycontin pain pills and popped them both in his mouth. He rinsed them down with faucet water and looked at Young Hollywood. Before speaking, he walked through the remainder of the bathroom, looking underneath the stall doors to make sure no one else was in there. After he checked the four stalls, he went back to the sinks and wall mirror and stood beside Young Hollywood.

"Strength comes in numbers, pimp." He looked at him through the mirror.

"Meaning?" Young Hollywood asked. Although he'd heard the quote several times before in his life, he really wanted to hear what Six Nine had to say.

"Meaning, I got a clique of goons nearly one hundred deep, and respect for my city and niggas from the A."

Young Hollywood looked confused, not clearly understanding where Six Nine was going with the small talk. "I'm still not quite understanding your meaning."

"When y'all was shootin' the video for Mossburg over there on the Westside, and when I got word that the New Orleans cats had shot up the video set, I sent some of my niggas over there immediately." He paused and took a deep breath, then he went on. "I knew ya'll thought that we, as the Black Cartel, had ordered the hit."

"That's the past, shawty. We got to the bottom of it, we cliqued. We got rid of the problem. I'm convinced."

"Yeah, you may be convinced, but what 'bout Hammer?"

Young Hollywood managed a smile. "My old man speaks highly of you. As a matter of fact, he's been appointed as your trial attorney."

Now Six Nine looked confused. Staring through the wall mirror, from behind him he noticed three men in suits enter the bathroom. Kangoma was the only one who didn't wear a mask. The other two armed men appeared to be trained; they wore badges around their necks as if they were police.

Kangoma placed plastic restraints on Young Hollywood's

wrist in the front. Six Nine couldn't believe what was going on. Now, with the gunmen aiming their mini assault rifles at him, Kangoma placed another plastic set of restraints on Six Nine.

Kangoma addressed them both in a calm manner. "Gentlemen, we're gonna walk out of here as if y'all are being arrested. Don't look at no one, don't try to say anything to anyone."

Six Nine laughed aloud, knowing this was all a joke. He'd had goons inside the restaurant and in the parking lot. At least that's what he thought. Everybody had been deleted or either removed from their post. Six Nine looked over at Young Hollywood, his head slowly shaking side to side.

"The games niggas play in da city." His eyes were deadly as he growled.

When Kangoma ushered Young Hollywood through the bathroom door and out into the restaurant, the other two goons got on either side of Six Nine.

They escorted him out as well.

29

Nearly forty minutes passed. The night skies were dark, but highlighted from a half moon that seemed to be glowing over the ranch home of Nicole Terry. Young Hollywood rode on the passenger side of a tinted Suburban. Kangoma drove, with his eyes darting from the mouth of the entrance gate and into the rearview. In the rear, Six Nine sat quietly in handcuffs and shackles clamped around his ankles, surrounded by three goons who were armed and well dressed.

When Six Nine finally decided to say something, his words came low and raspy. "Damn, pimp. Dis how yawl niggas playin' the game?"

Young Hollywood never turned to face him, but in a venomous tone, he said, "Your life could be redeemed, but if it was up to me... If it had been my call, yo bitch ass would've been dead."

"Damn! Now I'ma bitch?" Six Nine asked.

"You'll get your chance to prove otherwise."

Kangoma was easing through the gate now, and the only thing that could be heard was the roaring Chevrolet engine underneath the hood. Twisting and turning down the winding driveway, they rode past the main estate and toward the huge guesthouse. The headlights danced and moved across several parked cars and SUVs. Kangoma parked, and before he could switch off the engine, Young Hollywood had already opened his door and stepped down. Slamming the door behind him, he disappeared into the dark.

When Kangoma switched off the engine, he stepped out from the SUV, walked to the rear, and opened the door where Six Nine was waiting. He swung his shackled legs around first; his eyes bored into Kangoma's eyes, realizing Young Hollywood had sold him a damn good and straight-faced lie. When Kangoma reached inside his jacket with one swift motion, Six Nine braced himself for a bullet. Instead, Kangoma removed a single key, grabbed the chain, and unlocked the shackles.

Six Nine jumped down and towered over Kangoma. Kangoma stood in front of him, looking up into his eyes. Six Nine's face was relaxed, as the other three goons spilled from the SUV, still laced in ski masks and armed. They took their position, one of them in the front, leading Six Nine to his destiny. The other two played the back.

Kangoma removed the plastic restraints from his wrist and said, "Okay, here's the business. You follow us in here, I'll direct you to your seat. Once seated, the judge will enter and you will rise."

Six Nine laughed.

Kangoma even flashed a smile himself and patted Six Nine on his back.

Inside the house, which was set up and decorated like a courtroom, there were fifteen rows of pews lined on one side and fifteen lined on the other side, leaving room for a carpeted aisle. The pews were filled with nearly sixty men and women, all dressed in black tuxedos. Each person was a top official in Hammer and the Governor's organization. The majority of the men were in their late forties and early fifties, ex killers and assassins. Each was a millionaire and married to highly loyal and educated women.

The few women that were sprinkled through the audience were between the ages of thirty and fifty years old. Each of them strong, independent and college graduates.

To the left of the room was the jury box, segregated in a section of wood walls with twelve young black jurors of Six Nine's peers. Evenly separated, there were six men and six women, dreads, gold teeth with diamonds, bloodshot eyes for some of them, marijuana scent reeking from their breath and clothes. The majority of them were on something, ranging from pills and marijuana to heroin and cocaine. And of course, everyone had a felony on their record.

When Six Nine finally entered, escorted by Kangoma, they actually stopped. Six Nine studied his surroundings and mentally captured the entire room. He couldn't believe the set up. *Just like a muthafuckin' courtroom,* he said to himself and slowly shook his head. None of the faces in the pews was familiar to him. He felt Kangoma's fingers on the small of his back, urging him to walk forward.

Six Nine moved forward, walking up the aisle. Looking toward the left, he noticed the jury and actually flashed a smile. Now he was being directed to an oak wood table with two comfortable chairs. One of the chairs was his.

"Have a seat," Kangoma told him. "Your attorney will be out in a minute."

Six Nine took the seat further to the right. He looked up at Kangoma, his eyes were becoming more alert now. "Who my attorney?" he asked.

Kangoma looked back over his shoulder as he walked the front, and said, "Hammer Cocharan." Then he went through the side door.

Small chatter and whispering filled the courtroom and Six

Nine began to stress a little. He didn't have a clue whatsoever about what was going on.

Hammer emerged from the side door in a dark gray tailored suit and a briefcase. He went directly to the table where Six Nine was sitting and sat down next to him, placing the briefcase on the table. Physically, Hammer seemed to have fully recovered from his ordeal, but the haunted look in his eyes showed that he was still grieving for the loss of Atiya and Nzile.

Hammer looked at him with a smile and extended his hand for Six Nine to shake.

Six Nine refused the handshake and stared at Hammer. "What the fuck is all this shit about?"

"Jury trial. I'll be defending you."

"Man, y'all fuck niggas might as well gon' kill me now." He spoke quietly, so that only Hammer could hear him.

Hammer took a deep breath. "This is a serious matter. I'm really defending your life. That's on my word."

"Defending my life against who?" He was angry now.

Just then, Young Hollywood emerged from the side door with Sasha on his heels. They went to the table across from them. Six Nine laughed to himself. He couldn't believe what he was seeing. They took a seat at the table, never even looking in the direction of Hammer and Six Nine.

Sasha lifted a briefcase to the top of the table, laid it flat and flipped it open. Young Hollywood finally looked in Hammer and Six Nine's direction, and with his face as calm as possible, he slowly raised his hand and turned it into the shape of a pistol.

Hammer leaned into Six Nine. "That's the district attorney we'll be fighting against."

Six Nine rose to his feet. Hammer did also, just in case he wanted to try something stupid. Instead, he yelled across the room at Young Hollywood. "Nigga, we been handlin' shit in the streets." He looked around at the visitors in the courtroom, his face twisted and angry.

"At least you got a jury of your peers.

"Fuck you, nigga."

"Nah, you got to fuck ya bitch, pimp." Young Hollywood said calmly.

Just then, an alarm went off inside Six Nine's head. He'd forgotten about his fiancée, Amber. He looked at Hammer, his eyes squinting. "Where the fuck is Amber?"

30

H ammer looked up at Six Nine and noticed the deadly stare in his eyes, Six Nine was breathing hard, and Hammer could see his chest rising and falling. The desperation in his eyes told Hammer that he was ready to do something stupid. Hammer looked over at Kangoma where he was standing off to the side. They made eye contact, then Hammer nodded.

Kangoma turned and went through side door. It didn't take him a full minute to reappear with Amber alongside him, her eyes giving off pain and despair. She walked inside the courtroom with her arms folded across her chest, her legs chopping like scissors as she approached Six Nine. His demeanor changed just at the sight of her, and the closer she got, the harder his heart beat.

When she finally got to him, their arms nearly spread in unison. For a moment, his eyes closed and he actually fought back tears that had begun to creep up. Amber's arms were wrapped underneath his, her head pressed against his chest, and his head was pressed against the top of hers. When she raised her head and looked up at him, her eyes filled with tears.

"Don't cry, baby," Six Nine whispered in her ear. A lump formed in his throat and it seemed as if they were in their own world, standing in the middle of their own spacious living room floor.

At that moment, a voice yelled, "All rise."

Six Nine looked up as everyone shuffled to their feet. His head and eyes aimed toward the front of the courtroom. The Judge climbed the steps from the rear, and slowly, his head and face became clearly visible.

Six Nine looked at the man who was much older than him, and did not recognize his face. He wore a crisp pin stripe suit and a huge pinky ring that was flooded with diamonds and rubies. When he stared around at the crowded courtroom, his face finally registered as the Governor of the streets of Atlanta. Just then, Kangoma came over to separate Amber from him. His stare hardened when he looked at Kangoma.

Amber was led to an available seat on the bench three rows behind him.

Before the Governor said one word, he stood and stared around the courtroom while removing a cigar from his inner jacket pocket along with a lighter, and lit it. The smoke danced around his face and slowly faded up toward the ceiling. When he sat down, he motioned for everyone else to be seated as well.

They all found their seats, and the Governor adjusted the microphone. His eyes settled in on Hammer and Six Nine for a brief second, then they shifted toward Young Hollywood and Sasha at the prosecution table. From there, he looked at the dysfunctional jurors. The guy with his entire face covered with tattoos and a mouth full of gold teeth was the most noticeable person. He just shook his head in disbelief and wondered what the world was coming to.

"Street courts of Atlanta is in session." He puffed one time on his cigar and set it in the waiting glass ashtray, and then he picked up his gavel and hit the wooden block. He gave Young

Hollywood a nod, telling him to proceed and introduce the case.

Young Hollywood stood up, walked from behind the table, and took the floor. "Good evening ladies and gentlemen, majority of you know me as Young Hollywood. I'm the active prosecutor in this death penalty case. This trial will be based on pure facts and street credibility. No hearsay whatsoever." He paused, turned directly toward Six Nine, and stared him in his eyes. Then he pointed. "This man is a threat to the streets of Atlanta, to our wives and mothers, and most importantly, our children. For the record, your honor and the streets of Atlanta, this man has murdered at least six women and kids."

Hammer stood up. "Objection, your honor."

The Governor looked at him. "On what grounds?" The old raspy voice boomed through the surround sound speakers hidden inside the walls.

Hammer couldn't believe it. *On what grounds?* He repeated the words to himself. Staring at the Governor, he shook his head. "My client is from the streets of Atlanta, we simply had a word of agreement that if you were from Atlanta and born in Grady, that we wouldn't seek the death penalty."

Six Nine was listening more closely now. He was actually believing that this was real, and not some off the wall dream he had before when he was high on pills and codeine cough syrup. It seemed as if everything had gotten quiet while the courtroom waited for the Governor's response.

The Governor looked at Young Hollywood and Hammer, and called them both up to the bench. His huge hand covered the microphone as he leaned up and whispered, "If we're gonna keep it street official, let's keep it street official." His eyes cut into Young Hollywood.

Young Hollywood wasn't satisfied, but he'd kept his word with Hammer and the Governor that he'd keep everything clean. With a small attitude, he shrugged, turned around and went back to his table. He sat down next to Sasha and whispered something in her ear.

She listened intently, nodded then she stood up and walked toward the rear of the courtroom. She noticed Amber's cold stare, but she ignored her and continued moving outside.

The Governor sat back. "Who's the first witness?"

Young Hollywood spread his hands. "Ain't no witnesses in street court, remember?" Then he stood up. "But I would like to call Six Nine to the stand."

Hammer whispered to Six Nine, "You wanna go up there and explain your side of the story?"

In a cold tone of voice, he said, "I don't owe nobody no muthafuckin' explanation." Then out of anger, he snapped up to his feet and walked toward the witness stand.

Everyone had a shocked expression on their faces. Young Hollywood gave a surprised look himself, with a hidden smile that was cold and chilling.

The Governor held out a leather bound Bible, and when Six Nine placed his hand on it, the Governor looked at the missing finger then he looked Six Nine in his eyes. "Raise your right hand."

He raised it.

"Do you swear to tell the truth, the whole truth, and nothing but the truth, so help you God?"

Six Nine responded. "Fuckin' right."

Small chatter and laughter came from the audience as Six Nine took a seat in the witness box and situated himself. His eyes found Amber; her eyes were sad and puffy. His heart tightened inside his chest at the thought of her safety. Amber was the first woman that he'd desired to spend the rest of his life with. His eyes moistened, then his stomach muscles tightened. The more he looked into her eyes, the softer his heart became. Then she covered her face with her hands and broke down in tears.

Six Nine looked at the Governor. "Free her for me, and I'll plead guilty."

Young Hollywood read his lips and stood up. "No negotiations, pimp." He moved to the center of the floor and went with the first question.

"Are you the leader of the Black Cartel?"

"The Black Cartel doesn't operate under a leader. We're brought to you by the streets of Atlanta."

"Well, from my understanding, the Black Cartel was formed and established by you, the infamous Six Nine, while on the seventh floor of Rice street county jail."

"Okay, let's say I did start it." Six Nine snapped. "Now what?"

Just then, Sasha entered the courtroom with two champagne glasses and a bottle of Ace of Spade. When she got to the prosecution table, she popped the top on the bottle and poured up the two glasses. Young Hollywood took his glass and toasted with Sasha. He turned and faced Six Nine. He took a quick sip, then he asked, "Was the Black Cartel formed to over throw A-Town Records and Studio?"

Hammer stood up. "Objection, your honor. A-Town Records shouldn't be brought up whatsoever."

The Governor looked at the court and the jurors. "Disregard that last question."

Young Hollywood looked a Hammer and gave him a smile, while shaking his head. Then he turned toward Six Nine. "In the last three years, what have you done positive for the streets of Atlanta?"

Six Nine smiled for the first time. "I've killed numerous snitches for the streets of Atlanta, and robbed several out-of-towners that thought they was gonna come on my turf and take over."

Amber froze, this time she felt pain and grief that was unbearable.

Young Hollywood nodded slowly, appearing to be impressed with his answer. Then he asked, "How many children have you killed?"

"Excuse my language to the ladies and the court. But I'm a man of respect, if you wanna call me jackin' my dick in the privacy of my home killin' kids, then so be it."

Young Hollywood was burning up on the inside. He could end it all right here, right now. One single bullet underneath his ribcage and watch him die a slow death. However, he'd given Hammer and the Governor his word that he would keep everything clean. Young Hollywood turned up the glass and took a sip while standing in the center of the floor. "No further questions, your honor."

31

The Governor's eyes shifted toward Hammer and he leaned into the microphone.

"You got anything?" he asked him.

When Hammer stood up and took the floor, it seemed that all eyes were directly on him. He carried a full sheet of notebook paper with him, nothing more. Standing directly in front of Six Nine, he unfolded it and reviewed his notes. With a sharp memory, he etched everything in his head and eased the paper into his inside jacket pocket. He looked to the Governor and bowed his head slightly. Then he turned and looked at Young Hollywood and Sasha, neither of them looked happy, but in his eyes, they did look good together.

He gave them a brief nod, and then he proceeded. "Six Nine, in the course of your criminal career, could you give the court a rough estimate of how much money you've given to the streets of Atlanta?"

Six Nine cleared his throat. He seemed a bit more relaxed now, and even more eager to answer a simple question as this one. "First of all, I've supported all the local drug dealers around the city. I've bought pounds of Kush, pounds of Midget. I've spent probably a quarter million dollars with the young crew on x-pills." He paused and looked at the jury box. Every set of eyes were directly on him, then he asked, "Anybody familiar with the x-men over on Boulevard?"

Three hands went up from the jury box. A female with a silver piercing in her bottom lip blurted out, "Hell yeah, X-men keep the best pills in town." She turned up a warm orange juice and added, "Shid, I'm rolling now."

Then came snickers and low laughter from the remainder of the jurors and some of the audience as well. Governor banged his gavel two quick times and everything was quiet again.

Hammer continued his questioning. "Anything else positive you've done for the streets that you'd like to share with us?"

"Listen, pimp," Six Nine began counting on his fingers, starting with his pinky. "Magic City... Nikki's... Gentlemen Club... Strokers... Blue Flame... Pin Up... Pink Pony... Follies." He paused for a moment, and then said, "I've supported these businesses, I've supported the bitches that dance and sell pussy, and then I went even further. It's been several females that I just blessed when they need small shit like houses, cars and furniture. Man, I fuck with the city fa'real." He said in an arrogant tone and folded his arms across his chest.

When he made his last statement, Young Hollywood was sipping from his glass with his eyes fixed dead on Six Nine. Young Hollywood gave a smirk and twisted his mouth in one corner as if to say, 'Yeah, right.'

Young Hollywood had done his homework on Six Nine since he'd been home. He knew his strengths, and of course, his weaknesses as well. He knew his whole life, and he definitely could've murdered him a while back, several times over, but someone presented a better idea to him.

He stood up and looked at Hammer. "Are you through?" he asked calmly.

Hammer gave him a nod, walked back to the defense table, and sat down.

When Young Hollywood took the floor, he had a cheerful smile on his lips, as if he had something up his sleeve. He looked at his watch; it was seven minutes to ten. The night was still young, but he wanted to go ahead and get this over with. The crowd was older and needed their rest, so was the Governor. It was time to wrap this up.

Young Hollywood finally scanned the jurors and the audience. Some of the faces were tired and drained, and even he was feeling fatigued. When his eyes found one of the twins amongst the audience, he winked at him.

The twin stood up, dressed in a crisp gray three-piece suit. He moved toward the front of the prosecutor table, unzipped the bag in front of Sasha and removed a small recording device and a few more pieces of hi-tech surveillance equipment.

The crowd looked on quietly as Apple Head set everything up. He ran a wire to a twin set of base speakers. When he finished, he looked at Young Hollywood and gave him a nod that everything was ready.

That's when Young Hollywood clapped his hands three times. "To the court, and ladies and gentlemen of the jury. What I'm about to present to you is a recorded phone conversation between Six Nine and another member of his notorious Black Cartel. So everybody should listen closely and pay attention to the conversation." He walked back to his table and sat down next to Sasha. After he sipped from his glass again, he finally pressed play on a small Hi-tech recorder. The first voice that came through the speakers was Six Nine.

"Pimp, these niggas runnin' 'round here like they own the city.

And since this nigga, Young Hollywood, dun came home, I'm supposed to let up the pressure."

"No, you don't suppose to let up the pressure. Apply it full throttle if you want. But to avoid another war, and to be able to walk through the city without having to watch your back every five minutes..."

"I think you missin' the point. I'm three steps ahead of these monkey ass niggas. I got tracking devices on these niggas' cars. I know where they lay their head. I know how long these niggas be fuckin their bitches, and better yet, I got an inside nigga who do exotic food dishes. If I don't kill this nigga Hamma this year... Somebody in his family gots to get it. Especially that pretty ass Arab bitch. I'd love to slam dunk some pimpin in her ass. I'll sho nuff be the king of the city if I get that nigga, Young Hollywood, out the way. You feel me, pimp?"

"Fuckin right."

Young Hollywood pressed the stop button and the only sounds that could be heard were small whispers and chattering amongst the jurors and the remainder of the court. He stared at Six Nine with sharp intelligent eyes.

Six Nine's eyes turned red with anger then he shifted his glance toward Hammer, who was already watching him with a cold and intense stare. He began writing something on a piece of paper. Then, Six Nine's eyes went to Amber. His heart tightened immediately inside his chest when he looked into her eyes. She was nearly in tears again, and to avoid his stare, she buried her face in her hands.

The courtroom was beginning to get louder, and the Governor quickly stood to his feet and everything got quiet. He looked toward Six Nine. "You can step down now."

When Six Nine stood up, he stretched and yawned, which was faker than an eight dollar bill. He was seriously thinking about grabbing the Governor in a chokehold, but he knew

Hammer had planned this out ten steps ahead, and he wouldn't have a chance in hell.

When he finally stepped down and went back to his seat, the Governor sat back down. "Any more witnesses for the defense?"

With an undecided head shake, Hammer knew all this was coming to an end, and whatever the jury would decide was the correct decision for Six Nine.

If they found him guilty, they would kill him tonight. And if they found him not guilty, the committee would have to let him walk out a free man. That agreement was not only written in blood, but etched in stone amongst the heads of the other organizations that were scattered across the city of Atlanta. That structure was becoming more popular, like the many mafias that were spread throughout New York and Chicago. Atlanta was catching up rapidly with the trend.

When the Governor turned his stare toward Young Hollywood, he saw in his eyes that Young Hollywood had something extravagant under his sleeve, something that would seal and approve a guilty verdict. "Do you have any more witnesses?" The Governor asked him.

Slowly, Young Hollywood stood. He moved to the middle of the floor and looked into the many faces of the court, and then his eyes scanned every face in the jury box. Some of them were high, and some were down-right bored and probably hadn't paid attention to one damn word.

Using his eyes to instill fear, "Make the right decision," was all he said. He looked toward the Governor and slowly shook his head.

The Governor stared directly towards the jury box, his hard red-veined eyes touching each of them individually. "Do y'all understand the circumstances of this trial?"

They all nodded their heads.

The Governor checked his watch. "Y'all got ten minutes to come up with a verdict."

The members of the jury pulled together in a circle. They chatted quickly, then a female stood up with dreads hanging past her shoulders.

"Not guilty."

32

Young Hollywood felt his stomach turn in knots. He twisted his face and turned to face the jury. The audience went into a frenzy.

Six Nine stood to his feet with a smile and began clapping his hands.

Hammer stood with him, his face unemotional. He extended his hand out toward Six Nine and he shook it.

Out of nowhere, a woman screamed out, "Noooo." Amber stood up in a rage, desperately trying to get to Six Nine.

Kangoma grabbed Amber; she was stronger than he thought. "You can't let this muthafucka go." She yelled hysterically, tears streaming down her face.

Six Nine was confused now, stopping in his tracks and staring at his fiancé in disbelief. Guns were drawn and aimed at her, while Kangoma and one of the twins were holding her away from Six Nine.

"He's guilty." She yelled again. She fell to her knees in tears, covered in perspiration.

Young Hollywood walked over to her and knelt down beside her. "Amber, what's wrong?"

Amber, still in a rage and shaking uncontrollably, raised her head and looked at Young Hollywood and then to Hammer. Her eyes darted around, and then she finally whispered, "He murdered my brother... He don't deserve to be set free."

"How do you know this?" Young Hollywood asked.

Her statement confused everyone. The woman that was supposed to be Six Nine's fiancée was now ready for him to die.

Then Hammer asked, "What the fuck are you talking about?"

When Amber looked around again, her eyes had turned deadly. The courtroom was silent as she whispered, 'I am Ambassador Black... The head of the New Orleans syndicate."

Young Hollywood turned and looked at Hammer, who seemed to be in shock. "Well, I be damn." he said to him. Then he turned and looked at the Governor. "Your Honor, I think we got a new witness," he said, and rubbed his hands together anxiously.

"The case is over." He shot back to Young Hollywood. "If anything, we ought to give her ass the death penalty for claiming to be Ambassador Black."

The room fell silent again. Young Hollywood looked at Six Nine and then to the girl, Amber, in pure disgust. He knew who she was, and so did Sasha. Now everyone in the court-room was looking at Young Hollywood, anxiously watching him.

In one quick motion, he pulled out a .45 and aimed it at Six Nine. When that happened, his men pulled out their weapons as well.

Six Nine smiled at him, then he said, "Come on with all this emotional ass shit, potna."

"You jammed, nigga. And I gave my word, but the only way you can leave here is running and on feet." He aimed the gun at the ground and let off one single round. The gun roared and the shell landed by Young Hollywood's feet.

Six Nine's face turned into a hard frown as he stared Young Hollywood dead in his eyes.

Kangoma came around and stood between Six Nine and Young Hollywood. He looked at Six Nine and said, "You free to go. But the only way you can leave is running out back through the woods."

Six Nine nodded and headed toward the door. Young Hollywood walked behind him until he got out the door.

It was dark outside, and the thick bushes led to the woods just behind them. Six Nine took off running through the trees and bushes, and Young Hollywood just stood there until he faded from his eyesight. He put his gun back in his waistline and went back inside where Hammer and the Governor were now standing around Amber.

Other members of their circle were setting up the tables and bringing out all types of exotic food and drink. They were about to eat and enjoy themselves.

Young Hollywood pulled his father and the Governor to the side away from everyone else. "What do we do with her?" he asked.

Hammer shrugged and said, "Far as I'm concerned, we can kill her. But who knows? I may have a change of heart after I eat."

The Governor stood quietly, his eyes moving from one to the other. He held his tongue and walked over to the tables that were now set in one long row.

———

Outside, Six Nine jogged through the night and through the dense trees. Just up ahead, he could see the headlights of cars and trucks on 285. He was smiling and tired, all at the same time, because he knew he'd gotten away again. "Fuck niggas ain't got no power in this city," he said to himself.

Just then, his left foot stepped into a real bear trap. "Shhiit!" He yelled out in pain and bent over to check it. Then he heard someone say something in a foreign language. He looked up, and to his surprise, one of the African child soldiers was standing there holding a razor sharp machete.

He swung it just below Six Nine's calf of the leg that was in the Bear trap. The leg was now hanging.

Six Nine yelled out in pain, and immediately went into shock. "Run," whispered the young soldier.

Six Nine's eyes were wide with fear. He tried to get up, but he felt another machete slice at his other leg and then another one chopping at his arm. His blood was spilling into the ground and he wasn't even able to scream anymore. The three African child soldiers were on him and chopping him into pieces. They picked up his limbs as they removed them. His head was the last thing that they severed.

This was an order that came straight from Young Hollywood. He'd gone against his word, and for the sake of his father, he didn't care. He still had his own motto, *a sucker will never be prehistoric.* He knew that one day soon, there would be other teams and circles who would emerge from the underground to seek revenge, or try to remove him and his family. But until then, the city of Atlanta belonged to him.

UNTITLED

Special Thanks to my Readers
Jessica Hooper L.A. Crenshaw District
Jaton Lozano Chi Town
Jamiske Jackson
Carrie Lattyak Youngstown, OH,
Schawanna Morris Sandusky, OH,
Tyesha St. Louis,
Danielle Richardson Charleston, NC
Lissha Sadler Detroit Michigan,
Katherine Kat Daily
Jennifer Williams Illinois,
Camesha Bailey Barbados
Latrenda Perkins Chicago
Tiffany Harris Kansas City, MO,
Tiffany Lewis Jones Chi Town
Diane C Locker PA
Shine South Carolina
Shanetra Miles-Fowler Chicago
Amy Juice Salmon Pittsburgh, PA
Dawn Cupcakegirl Jay Akron, OH

Chenelle Parker New Orleans
Shawn Stewart Camps Rock Hill, South Carolina
Melissa Bell
Janisha Houston, TX
Nikki Hamlet San Antonio
M... Debose C Town
Ebony Smith Palm Beach
Kira Mike Marietta, GA
Sherri Decatur, GA
Tanechea Merida Temple, Texas
Desiree Boomer Greensboro, North Carolina
Delores Miles Virginia
Consuella Shaw Lawrenceville, GA
Cassandra Imes Rochester, NY
Swipe DC
Victoria Madison, WI
Jae Garvin Milwaukee, WI
Rochelle Detroit, MI
Justin Alexander H-Town
Chapel Hill North Carolina
Lisa Hulon Wells Chapel Hills, NC
Quan Landa Chicago
Juanesia VA
Penney Gant Kansas City, MO
Stacey Parker Detroit, Michigan
Rebecca Ortiz San Francisco, CA
Shamika Smith Pittsburgh, PA
Creola Varnville, SC
Erika Newman Aiken, SC
Tamisha Taylor, Los Angeles
Regina Pouncy Calumet City
Kolette Jones Salisbury, MD
Nicole Cruz Palmdale
Kosha Jordon Gulf Port, Mississippi

Ronald Thomas Philly, South Jersey
Royal Crown Readers Cleveland, OH
Tricia Pratt Erie, PA
Triece Hanskins Savannah, GA
Nosha Peterson Long Beach, CA
Monica Fleming Fontana, CA
Smith Sharlene, Atlanta, GA
556 Book Chicks Atlanta, GA
Stacey Massey Montgomery, AL
Snow Camp NC
Karen Smith Detroit, MI
Mario Clark Norfolk, VA
Lois LoveJoy Columbus, GA
Kristy Bluitt Long Beach, CA
Jamerial Knight Montgomery AL
Rocky Mount, NC
Charlene Dixon Augusta, GA
Theresa Bawss Brown Rocky Mount, NC
Kenya Anthony Tennessee
Kya Brooklyn, NY
Rhea Alexis M Banks Chicago, IL
Charmaine Lovett Brunswick, GA
Kim Turner Buffalo, NY
Sarita Bush ATL
Kawand Da Don Crawford Brooklyn, NY
Yvette Edenton, Carolina
Kitani Martin Sumter, SC
Shirlyn Marshall Tupelo, MS
Ms. Antoine Lee, Richmond, VA
Meka Brown Mesquite, TX
Monique Williams Chicago
Wanda Chi Town
Vanessa Speaks Cleveland, Ohio
Terri Bawss Ellis Winooski, VT

Bettey Dukes Waynesboro, GA
Brenda Allen Long Beach, CA
Alterick Gaston Wilson, NC
Robin Rembert Inkster, MI
Keisha Noel Lauderhill, FL
Nicole Williams Atlanta GA